LT-W Paine

Paine, Lauran

Sixshooter Trail

SIXSHOOTER TRAIL

Lauran Paine

CHIVERS
THORNDIKE

This Large Print book is published by BBC Audiobooks Ltd, Bath, England and by Thorndike Press®, Waterville, Maine, USA.

Published in 2005 in the U.K. by arrangement with Golden West Literary Agency.

Published in 2005 in the U.S. by arrangement with Golden West Literary Agency.

U.K. Hardcover ISBN 1–4056–3402–2 (Chivers Large Print)
U.K. Softcover ISBN 1–4056–3403–0 (Camden Large Print)
U.S. Softcover ISBN 0–7862–7607–X (British Favorites)

The text of this Large Print edition is unabridged.
Other aspects of the book may vary from the original edition.

Set in 16 pt. New Times Roman.

Printed in Great Britain on acid-free paper.

British Library Cataloguing in Publication Data available

Library of Congress Cataloging-in-Publication Data

Paine, Lauran.
    Sixshooter Trail / by Lauran Paine.
        p.   cm.
    "Thorndike Press large print British favorites."—T.p. verso.
    ISBN 0–7862–7607–X (lg. print : sc : alk. paper)
    1. Texas—Fiction. 2. Large type books. I. Title: Sixshooter
    Trail II. Title.
    PS3566.A34S543 2005
    813'.54—dc22   2005003474

LT-W

Chapter One

There was a warped and grey-weathered shack in the canyon which blended so perfectly with its background of grey stone, dusty trees and ragged old sky that until the horse under him lifted his ears Hyatt didn't see it.

For that matter he'd very nearly missed that secret canyon altogether. It was one of those narrow, tree-choked places where a little sluggish run of water went silently downcountry southward from some distant and unknown source.

There was no real trail down into the little canyon either; there were a dozen different game trails heading for that water, for chokecherries and wild plums which grew along the creek-banks, but there was no actual man-trail at all. But if there had been the chances were excellent Hyatt wouldn't have used it. He wasn't in search of human companionship particularly when he spotted the roofline, the rafter-ends, and the soiled old door of that hidden cabin.

Still, he was down in that canyon now; he was twenty feet from that cabin where it lay westerly behind two enormous and very old oak trees, and if there was a man inside that shack, by now he'd have heard Hyatt—would have him beaded-in down the barrel of a

1

Winchester or a Colt. It paid, under these circumstances, for a man to move slowly but to think fast. It also paid him to act natural and keep his right hand well clear of his hip-holstered .45.

Hyatt did not, however, immediately dismount. He permitted his animal to shake down the reins, drop his head and drink creek-water. After that Hyatt tried his best to find that levelled gun in the weeds and trees and underbrush which hid the shack with their excellent camouflage. He didn't find it.

He swung down, splashed across the little creek leading his animal, looped the reins in tree-shade, then slowly walked on over to the cabin. For ten feet in front of that leather-hinged, dirty old door, the weeds had been scythed away. There was even a little bed of tended red geraniums near the front wall. Hyatt eyed those flourishing flowers, knelt and poked a finger into the ground. It was moist. He stood up, looked down the south wall and up the north wall. There was no rifle-barrel. He twisted from the waist gazing closely at every nearby weed patch and brush clump. Still no rifle-barrel.

Someone lived here; someone had recently watered those geraniums. But why? What could there possibly be in the bottom of a tree-shaded, secret little canyon to draw a man and to hold him there?

Hyatt heard a faint noise which could have

been human-made or animal-made. He stood stock-still listening, but it didn't come again.

The place was beginning to work on Hyatt's nerves, which were somewhat raw anyway. A Texas mid-summer scarcely had its devilish match anywhere on earth. But heat aside, Hyatt still had his reasons for also being down in this hidden place.

The sound came again, more whimper of despair than anything else. But in this close, hushed place with its echoing walls, its confining huge trees, its feeling of eyes everywhere, Hyatt could not place the source. He considered the shack's closed door, decided he'd go in there last; doors had habits of having armed men on the other side of them.

He stepped softly along the northward front wall of the cabin, turned where an intersecting wall came up, stepped twenty feet westward and came face to face with the solid rock face of a towering bluff of grey, lifeless stone. There were acorns underfoot that softly burst when Hyatt crushed them. There were also innumerable little sucker-oaks flourishing up out of the rotten stumps of bigger oaks which had been cut down several years earlier.

He re-traced his steps to the front yard again, walked southward down it to the other intersecting wall, went quietly along that until he came upon another, more ramshackle shed hidden farther back. Here, he found proof positive that someone had been in this place

3

only very shortly before he himself had arrived.

The smaller shed had a carefully contrived corral southward of it which blended so perfectly into the trees that Hyatt could follow it out only by picking up the first stringers and turning slowly as he traced them on out and around. Here, there was ample fresh horse-sign. Here too, there was a rumpled fresh bait of meadow hay in a manger. Hyatt walked up and gazed in; whoever he was, he hadn't been gone long. There were still wet ends where a horse had chewed on some of that hay.

He went up through the thicket, man-high and higher, pushing aside limbs, moving carefully now, not so sure that gun was tracking him now, but very curious and very interested. He stepped over close to the same abrupt-standing westerly bluff which formed one of the bulwarks of this secret place, and halted, for over here that rock was not as solidly resisting as it had been along its more northerly reaches. Here, Hyatt saw a grey and ragged old length of blanket hanging down. If he hadn't been within five feet of it though he'd never have spotted it. He knew, without even stepping across and lifting one edge of that old rag, what was back there.

A cave.

Not tall enough to stand fully erect in, and as dark as the inside of a well. But there was a candle-stub set in a hand-wrought old spiked holder, the kind miners used.

Hyatt felt no urge to explore this cave. Just by nature it went against Hyatt's grain to walk into anything as trap-like as this cave was certain to be. But he was none the less curious so he peered in, even took several steps inward behind the blanket.

The cave had to be very old. There was no slag heap where whoever had dug it had dumped their refuse. Moreover, the scrub-oak patch outside grew right up to the hole, even grew above it in rock-fissures.

The walls and overhead curved ceiling were smooth to the touch, no crumbly earth cascaded downward at the touch. There was a smell to the place Hyatt couldn't quite define; it had elements to it of old fires, of ancient cookery and animal fat. He returned to the heavy, hot and humid sunshine outside. The cave had been at least twenty degrees cooler, perhaps even more, and if nothing else made it inviting this did because summertime Texas was a bitterly, fiercely hot place.

He was gazing straight at the back-wall of the house. There was a window over there and another of those hand-made, worn-appearing old leather-hinged doors. From the direction he was looking came a long, sodden moan, and finally Hyatt placed the source of those other sounds he'd heard. Someone inside the house after all, and whoever that was, was in pain.

He waited a full minute after that sound died away. A man in a strange place got along best by minding his own business, and Hyatt's business right now was getting back to his horse; getting up out of this secret canyon he'd accidentally stumbled upon, and putting a lot of miles behind him.

The whimper came again. This time it sounded as though it was being dammed up behind clenched teeth, as though whoever was in there was perhaps stuffing a rag into their mouth to keep down the noise.

He'd be harmless, Hyatt told himself. A man didn't make sounds like those unless he was bad-hurt, perhaps dying, so whoever he was, he'd be harmless. Hyatt moved stealthily towards the window. But this was not a glass window as in the towns, this was one of those window-panes made of scraped clear rawhide which let in light in a murky, diffused way, but which were too opaque to see through.

He went along to the door, listened with his head down, made out the explosive breathing, the ragged sobs, and lay his left hand upon the draw-string, his right hand upon his sixshooter, and very gently opened the door.

It wasn't a man in there making those sounds, it was a woman—a girl, in fact, with a mass of very long, thick, wavy hair hanging sweat-dank; with a sweat-shiny face the colour of oily red clay all flushed and feverish, and

6

with enormous blue eyes the colour of columbine in early spring. She was biting her heavy underlip, staring straight at Hyatt from the rumpled wreckage of her bed, holding back a scream that made the veins in her neck stand out. She was swollen nearly twice normal size.

Hyatt stepped inside, closed the door and returned that pain-crazed stare. There wasn't much in the room; just that big bed where the wild-eyed straining girl lay, a black little old iron stove, several rickety chairs, a make-shift table, dresser, mirror with a crack its full length, and some other odds and ends; cupboards, a mound of tangled saddlery, several weapons placed in corners around the room, a washstand, and commode set of white china.

He stepped over to the girl. Her eyes were swollen from crying, her flushed face was unattractive from the strain of agony. Her hands and wrists were small but she was not a slight woman; she was long-legged and had at one time been willowy and tall. Now, she looked to Hyatt like a heifer which had been eating lupin; all swollen in the middle. She stared upwards, sometimes rational, sometimes defiant, sometimes dreadfully fearful and pleading.

A man such as Hyatt Tolson who had come to manhood among men, had no difficulty at all diagnosing this girl's trouble, but he'd never before been close to it either. She was in the process of having a baby.

He'd calved out his share of heifers and had helped at foaling time with fillies, but this was different; this was a woman, a human being. Still, as he told himself, *you're here and she's here and if there are no complications you can help her, because it's about like a heifer or a filly.*

He put aside his hat and saw her watching him. Neither of them said a word. He went to the basin, filled it with water with his back to her, washed hard and dried off, turned back and saw that her stare towards him had softened a little; most of the defiance was gone as though she understood. But she suddenly convulsed, bit hard down upon her lower lip again and gripped the rumpled blankets until the cords of her neck stood out as taut as bowstrings.

He moved over to her saying, 'Go ahead and yell. Cuss if you want to-let yourself go.'

She didn't though; she fought through that spasm as she'd obviously been fighting through others as bad for hours. When she was rational again and wildly panting, she looked up with a head-wag. 'I dassn't; they'll hear.'

'Who'll hear?' he asked, and gave his head a negative wag. 'Lady; this canyon's too far from anywhere for you to be heard. I just stumbled on to it myself.'

'No,' she whispered. 'Don't pretend. I know who you are. I know why you came here. But you won't get him. You or any of them. You'll never get him.'

'Lady, I don't want him—whoever he is. Like I said, I just ...'

She turned rigid; her mouth flew wide open without a sound coming out of it. She grabbed for something to hold to and her eyes bulged with a terrible straining. Hyatt stood like stone, watching until her breath burst explosively and her lips formed one word: Help!

He swung into action. He was a stocky, strong and confident man. He had a rudimentary knowledge of what must be done so he bent over and went to work. Sweat popped out upon his forehead and his upperlip; as the frightening moments ran on great crescents of perspiration appeared at his armpits. He was too engrossed in his work to hear anything outside, and even if he'd been listening, the girl's shattered breathing would have interfered.

Hyatt was not a praying man and he didn't pray now, but he *hoped*; hoped so hard it was the same as prayer. Hoped with all his fierce strength and will that there would be no complications.

The air in the shack was stifling-hot and rank. The girl's agony gradually subsided; she seemed to sink into a deep stupor. Her breathing was very lethargic, very shallow. There was a sluggish trickle of blood where

9

she'd bitten through her underlip. Outside in a tree a bluejay made its raucous cry of warning. Hyatt hardly heard the bird at all. He sank down upon the side of the bed drained of all his strength.

Chapter Two

There wasn't a sound outside after that bluejay made its outcry and fled southward down the canyon. Hyatt, with an instinctive knowledge, went through all the motions of bathing the baby in lukewarm water, in tenderly drying it, wrapping it in the cleanest rags he could find, and placing it, red and wrinkled and sluggishly moving, in a wooden box which had once held kindling shavings for the cook-stove.

After that he took fresh water to the bedside and bathed the girl. He was clumsy at this and sometimes rough, but he was sure it must be done. Not until he'd finished, was making a smoke with unsteady hands, did he let go. He was wrung out, drained dry of all strength and emotion. He was so dulled and limp that when the back door opened and a big, rough appearing man with several days' beard growth upon his sun-bronzed face stepped inside pointing a cocked sixshooter straight at Hyatt's middle, he didn't move.

The big man said nothing, he simply stood

10

over there with that dead-level gun as steady as rock in his fist, staring at Hyatt. Eventually he inclined his head a little.

'Shuck the sixshooter,' he quietly said.

Hyatt obeyed, dropping his gun to the floor. He'd never seen this big man before, had no idea who he was, but thought he was too old to be the girl's husband—if she had one—and was too coarse-featured to be her father.

The big man swung his eyes to the kindling-box where the baby was making snuffling sounds and jerky movements. He looked off on his left towards the bed and the wax-like girl over there with her upper body barely rising and falling. He looked back at Hyatt.

'What happened?' he asked, using that same quiet, Texas drawl.

'She had a baby,' explained Hyatt.

The big man's gunbarrel drooped a degree. 'The hell,' he said, sounding astonished. 'You delivered it?'

'Wasn't anyone else around, mister.'

The big man called back out through the doorway at his back. 'In here, fellers. I got him—I'm not sure he's the right one, but I got him. Come in here.'

Three other strangers walked up and pushed inside. Like the big man, these others were also unshaven and rough looking men with guns and flinty eyes and flat-held menacing lips. They fanned out in the room eyeing the girl, the baby, and Hyatt Tolson.

11

They seemed a little uncertain about their position, but not the least bit uncertain about Hyatt.

The big one put up his gun, tiptoed to the bedside and stood a moment gazing at the girl. When he turned, his gaze at Hyatt was a little less bitter.

'You made the right choice,' he said. 'I reckon even an outlaw like you's got somethin' inside him, when the chips're down, mister. It'd be hard, hanging a feller who give up his only chance to stand by his woman when she needed him bad, like this.' The big man looked at his companions. 'Let's take him in, boys; let's don't lynch him after all. He could've beat us out of the country; he could've left her here to whelp alone. I've always said, ain't a man livin' that's *all* bad.' The rough strangers looked back and forth. That big man was the eldest; he also looked to be the roughest. One of the others shrugged, eyeing the kindling-box.

'All right with me, Sim,' he muttered.

The other two nodded, saying nothing, also eyeing that crate with its mite of wrinkled new life in it. One of them stepped up to gaze downward. 'Sure little,' he murmured. 'Kind of ugly though, ain't he?'

Hyatt Tolman looked over. 'She,' he said. 'Not he. You fellers mind telling me what this is all about?'

The big man ran a soiled sleeve across his

12

sweated face and turned sardonic. 'Mister, let's don't play games. You hit the coach, got the money and shot the guard. We know it an' you know it.' Those sardonic grey eyes rested fully upon Hyatt. 'Get up and let's get goin'. It's a long way back to town.'

Hyatt got up and kept watching the man called Sim. It wouldn't help to deny he'd robbed a stage or shot anyone; not right now anyway. And there was an excellent chance that arguing might upset these tough-faced cattlemen—or whatever they were—turning them back to what had clearly been their original intention, and being lynched wasn't a pleasant prospect.

'What about her,' he said, nodding towards the bed. 'And her baby?'

'Take them too,' growled one of the other men. 'One of us can ride double, the others can take turns packin' the chile.'

'Be more humane,' said Hyatt to this man, 'to shoot her right here and bust the kid's skull against a tree-trunk like Indians do.'

Big Sim's steely eyes turned cold. 'What kind of talk is that?' he demanded of Hyatt Tolman. 'You just saved her life and the baby's life too; what kind of a man are you, mister?'

'A humane one,' replied Hyatt, returning Sim's look squarely. 'That girl's in no condition to travel. She had a bad time of it. She'll haemorrhage if you put her on a horse and bleed to death before you've gone five

13

miles. Then who'll feed the baby?'

Those four unkempt, unshaven men looked at one another, over towards the bed then back to Hyatt Tolman. Sim's look of antagonism faded a little as he considered what Hyatt had told him.

One of the others said, 'Likely he's right, boys. She's young an' she looks used up. One of us got to stay here until the others take this feller into town an' sends back old Doc Crump.'

Hyatt nodded at this man. 'That's the only solution, mister; are you goin' to be the one who stays?'

'I can,' stated the cowman, eyeing Hyatt with a faint-stirring wonderment in his stare. 'Anythin' special I got to know?'

'Yeah; she's feverish. Keep washin' her face and neck with cold water. When she comes around, give her the baby. It's got to suck the same as a newborn calf. If she's hungry, mix up some gruel or somethin' soft and nourishing.'

Sim said, 'Mister; why'd you drag her into this with you? Why didn't you leave her with her folks—if she's got any?' Sim gazed downward at the grey-faced girl and wagged his head. 'You should've waited 'til she done had the chile, mister, before you hit a stage. Hell; anyone with half an eye could see she couldn't ride hard'n fast with you, afterwards.'

Hyatt drew in a big breath, briefly held it, then let it out. He had his truthful answer to

14

Sim, but he didn't offer it, he said, 'Come on. If we're goin' let's get on the trail.'

Sim squared back around. He was a powerfully put-together man, well over six feet in height and better than two hundred pounds in heft. He had a good face, but coarse and rough and scored by many savage summers and hard winters. He was one of those frontier Texans who made a loyal friend and an implacable enemy. He jerked his head at Hyatt, 'Head for your horse, mister. Bud; you heard what you got to do until we can send Doc Crump back. Do it. An' don't tell her we got him; it'd only upset her more.'

'Sure,' assented the one called Bud. 'I understand.'

They already had Hyatt's horse, and as they herded him over to it, in among their own tucked-up, salt-caked and ridden-down beasts, Sim came up even with Tolman and shook his head with a morose expression on his unshaven face. 'The guard didn't die so maybe they won't hang you, but I got a feelin' your little daughter'll be half-growed before you set eyes on her again. That was federal money you stole, cowboy, and they send 'em to the Fort Leavenworth penitentiary for riflin' the gov'ment mail and makin' off with gov'ment money.'

Hyatt checked his cincha, stepped up over leather with the others around him, and said nothing. He hadn't robbed any coach or shot

15

anyone—stagecoach armed guard or anyone else—but he recognised the futility of trying to convince these rough men of that.

They didn't strike him as particularly bitter or vindictive men; simply as possemen doing their duty. They watched him, and clearly they'd kill him without compunction if they had to. They'd have hanged him in that secret canyon with the same impersonal sentiment too, except for that nameless girl back there and her baby, but they weren't cruel people.

Texas was a harsh place; had been for over a hundred years. Its environment formed and sustained harsh men. In avenging their hallowed dead at the Alamo, Texans had, in something like eighteen minutes, butchered four hundred Mexican soldiers at the Battle of San Jacinto when they'd won their independence from Mexico many years earlier.

Texas was not an easy place, neither in its way of life nor in the way it yielded up its resources to men and women who grubbed out their bleak existence there. Texans were an elemental people; like Sim and his companions, riding along with Hyatt Tolman towards the village of Canebrake, they knew right from wrong, good from bad, and did not compromise. They shot when they had to, hanged whom they had to, and resisted lawlessness, usually, with a blind-stubborn resistance born of the need for civilised people living together on a raw frontier, to remain

16

civilised regardless of the cost.

Hyatt understood Texans because he, too, was one. This west-Texas world of the big sky and the forage-grass plains was not his country though; he'd come to manhood up closer to Oklahoma—up nearer the Indian Nation. And Sim's talk of Fort Leavenworth had a familiar ring too. Hyatt Tolman had been there; had in fact, been riding in the opposite direction from Leavenworth penitentiary in as straight a line as he could, when he'd gone down into that secret canyon where a cruel Fate had called a sudden halt to the westerly flow of his destiny.

He was now riding southeastward, to some degree at least, back in the same direction he'd recently come. He'd come across no town, before, but even if he'd seen one he'd have avoided it. He had his personal reasons; there are times in the life of men when the postures, the structures, the scents and sights made by men are abhorred. That's how it had been with Hyatt Tolman ever since leaving Leavenworth up on the Kansas plains.

They crossed a rolling landswell where, from its gravelly crest, Hyatt first saw Canebrake. It wasn't much a town. There wasn't a tree within a mile of it; in summertime trees were friends to wandering riders. The buildings were raw and pitchy, unpainted and sun-bleached. Mostly, the rooftops were oiled wood, but here and there among the main-street stores was the fierce reflection of late-day, red sunlight off tin.

Canebrake was a dusty, parched place too. Scattered indiscriminately around it like unwashed urchins, lay shacks and cabins, adobe *jacals,* with an infrequent residence showing real glass windows and maybe a little picket fence. It was obviously a cow-town; Hyatt had seen his share of places resembling Canebrake. As he slouched along among his silent companions, he thought he'd also encountered his share of the kind of people he'd find here.

'Mister,' said big Sim, looking thoughtfully ahead at the town. 'There's bad feelin' in town, naturally. You can't expect anythin' else. But you can maybe help yourself a mite by takin' the law to wherever you cached that money-pouch.'

Hyatt rolled his head around to study Sim's deep-lined, square-jawed face. He said nothing. Around him the other men kept staring straight ahead as though they hadn't heard Sim speak. Texans were, under normal conditions, a dry, taciturn people.

'I figure it'd he'p you get out sooner, mister,' went on Sim. 'An' I reckon even a man like you's got feelin' for his young; if you lacked that, I figure you'd have abandoned her back there, and the chile.' Sim swung his head to meet Hyatt's gaze. 'I'm not a family man m'self; it's taken me twenty years just to get organised so I eat reg'lar. But I ain't no different from other folks, an' this is a rough country. 'Ain't no place for a young mother an' a little girl to grow up 'thout their pappy an' husban' around.' Sim's steely eyes, perpetually narrowed by blazing suns, did not turn soft or maudlin at all. He wasn't a soft man. But Simpson Franklin was a practical, even gentle man, in his own rough way.

'Let 'em have the lousy money, mister. If you don't—if you hold out an' keep it buried— by the time you get out it just might be there won't be nothin' in the world you'll be able to buy with it you'll be so old. Or else—who can say?—your girl an' your baby'll be—well—you know what I'm thinkin', because like I just said, this is a hard country. It's full of women-hungry men—an' worse.'

Hyatt's attention was caught by the distant high cry of some northward horsemen beating along southward towards Canebrake with a streamer of heavy dust flaring outwards in their wake.

'More of the posse,' muttered one of the men behind Hyatt. 'They seen we got someone.'

Sim lifted his rein-hand, watching those riders swerve to intercept him. 'Let's get a mite closer in,' he said, and booted his horse over into a shambling lope, his meaning starkly clear. Those other men, wrung out and disappointed, would be in no mood for taking Hyatt Tolman into Canebrake for the badge-toting law to handle in its slow and often bumbling manner.

The four of them covered a good long mile and were on the outskirts of town before the other riders even came close. By then it was too late for them to take matters into their own hands, if indeed that had been their intention. Still, they joined up with Sim and his friends just beyond the farthest outlying shacks and called sharp questions forward as they slowed to a hard trot, came in close and glared over at Hyatt Tolman. They, too, were rawboned, hard-faced, rugged men of the fierce border-country breed.

Sim and his friends gave short answers. Hyatt looked once at these other men, saw the resolution in their unfriendly faces, and prudently kept silent all the rest of the way into town.

Chapter Three

Canebrake lay in the county of Ellis. There was a Ranger post ninety miles northwest, up near the bad-lands, but unless requested by local authorities to do so, Texas Rangers rarely interfered in affairs which did not fall directly into their jurisdiction, or unless ordered into a locality by the Governor of Texas, whose office was in far off Austin.

20

Rangers frequently passed through Canebrake, and in fact there was one in town the evening Sim Franklin brought in Hyatt Tolman to be charged with the robbery of a south-bound stage, and the shooting of its armed guard. His name was Sam Hale. He was sitting with County Sheriff Tom Morse in Tom's front office down at the adobe jailhouse, relaxed and mildly attentive as Sheriff Morse explained about the stage holdup and the subsequent search for the outlaw.

Sheriff Morse, who had just returned from a hard ride under a murderous sun, was dusty, dehydrated, and feeling mean as a rattler. But he was by nature a gruff, tough man anyway, so the amount of profanity in his talk was only slightly more noticeable than usual, although the beet-red appearance of his face and the cracked condition of his lips attested to the hardship he'd endured this day as he said, 'Sam; you boys got to step in. That there was gov'ment money this feller stoled, and that there guard was a sort of gov'ment employee when this feller shot him.'

Hale, six feet tall and slightly under a hundred and fifty pounds in weight, was a long-legged, leaned-down, sinewy man about thirty years old. But he looked older and acted older, for like most Texans he'd had to mature fast in order to survive. All he said was: 'Tom; that'd be up to the gov'nor. You could write headquarters askin' for aid. You'd get it. But there's sure—Lord nothin' I can personally do. I'm just on my way back from a mighty hot an' dry sashay down along the border—a routine ride we always got to make when they's a rev'lution over in Mexico—which there always is in the summertime. You know, Tom, if I had my way I'd get a law passed that Messicans couldn't have no revolutions during June, July, August an' September. It's just plain too damned—'

The office door flew open, Sim Franklin pushing Hyatt Tolman ahead of him, walked in, and interrupted the rest of Sam Hale's remark. Sim nodded courteously at Hale, whom he didn't know from Adam's off ox, tossed Tolman's sixshooter down on Tom Morse's desk and said, 'Here's your stage robber.'

Sheriff Morse gazed steadily at Hyatt Tolman, looking him up and down. He didn't say a word. Ranger Hale, too, was interested, but the longer he looked the more baffled he seemed to also become.

Sim strode across to an earthen *olla*, tipped it, let cool water run down his gullet for a full minute, sighed loudly and moved back over where Tolman and the sheriff were appraising each other.

'He delivered a baby,' Sim said. 'That's how us to come on to him, Tom. If he'd abandoned his woman we'd never have caught him.'

22

'He . . . *A what?*' demanded Sheriff Morse, swivelling around to stare at Sim.

Sim Franklin explained all of it. The men with him back in the doorway, gravely kept nodding as Franklin talked. Behind these men were those other dusty, flinty possemen they'd encountered northwest of town. They were listening too, and looking just as dumbfounded and incredulous as Tom Morse was also looking.

As Sim finished he sauntered on closer to the door. 'I got to find Doc Crump an' guide him back there. I'll need a fresh horse, mine's plumb tuckered.'

'Wait a minute,' protested Tom Morse, getting to his feet. 'Sim; how'n hell do you know this here is the bandit?'

'Tracked him,' said Franklin succinctly. 'Picked up his sign where he stopped the coach, and tracked him arrow-straight down to that shack in the hidden gully. There weren't no other signs, Tom. This here is the right man, all right. Now I got to go find Crump.'

Franklin shouldered on out into the gathering skein of the lowering night. One of those men who'd been with Sim at the shack turned and followed him. The other two men were content to tiredly lean in the doorway gravely watching Sheriff Morse and Hyatt Tolman. Sam Hale, the Ranger, put a hand to his jaw and perplexedly stroked it. He was staring hard at Tolman.

Morse motioned doorward with a thick arm, 'Scatter,' he growled. 'Thanks for the help, boys. From here on the law'll take over.' Someone back in that crowd made an indistinguishably uncomplimentary comment about just what the law would really accomplish, then all those weary possemen began breaking up, drifting off through the pleasant roadway gloom.

Tom Morse went to the door, closed it, turned and brought his bushy brows together in a dark scowl at Tolman. 'Mister,' he said coldly, 'you're lucky. The guard'll live. All that means is that you're a lousy shot, even at close range, an' maybe it also means you won't get hung. But otherwise, you're in more trouble than a nest o' sinners at a prayer meetin'. What's your name?'

'Hyatt Tolman.'

The Ranger snapped his fingers and snapped up straight in his chair. Tom Morse looked around at him. 'You know him, Sam?' Morse asked.

'Been tryin' to recollect his name, Sheriff. It's sure'nough Hyatt Tolman.'

'Well,' growled the sheriff, 'he just told you that much, Sam.'

Hale put his pale eyes upon Hyatt. He made no further comment, just kept watching the prisoner, so Tom Morse resumed his questioning.

'Where's the money, Tolman; it might he'p

if you'd co-operate with the law.'

Hyatt turned, walked to a whittled little wall-bench, turned back and sat down upon it. He said, 'Sheriff; I'm not your stage robber. I was riding west, stumbled on to a shack in an arroyo, found a girl in there having a baby, helped her have it, and those fellers who brought me in rode up and threw down on me. That's the whole truth. I don't know anything about a stage holdup. I didn't even know this town was here. I was on my way out to California.'

'Sure,' said Tom Morse grittily. 'Sure you were, Tolman—with a pouch of gov'ment money.'

'With one hundred and seventeen dollars, Sheriff, which is still in my back pocket. That's every cent I own.'

Morse teetered up on to his heels then settled back down again. 'Have it your way,' he said, staring. 'I was just tryin' to show you a way things might go easier, Tolman. But have it your way. If we never find that money, you'll never see it again either. The law's got ways of bein' hard on fellers like you.'

Sam Hale finally spoke. Through all the exchange between Sheriff Morse and Hyatt Tolman he'd continued to assess the prisoner. Sam hauled up to his feet, hooked his thumbs in his shell-belt and gently wagged his head. 'Tom; before you go off half-cocked,' he said, 'let me step across the road an' send a telegram.'

Morse's expression, the longer he studied Hale, began to turn baffled and irritated. 'What for?' he finally demanded. 'You think this feller maybe ain't—?'

'No. No, Tom, nothing like that. I just don't think Hyatt Tolman's a stage robber. That's all.'

'Oh, you don't, don't you,' growled Morse. 'An' just what'n hell do you figure he is, Sam?'

'Well,' drawled the Ranger, 'I can tell you *part* of what he is, Tom. He's been in Leavenworth penitentiary up in Kansas since the war. He was one of those Confederate officers who wasn't covered by the general amnesty.'

Sheriff Morse, like all healthy Texans, had also been a Confederate soldier during the Civil War, and what Sam Hale said hit him hard, for, also like other Texans—the great majority of them—Tom Morse still had his secret sympathies. 'Him?' he said, furrowing his brow in powerful doubt. 'This here feller, Sam?'

'The same, Tom. What I want to know is just when Hyatt Tolman was released from Leavenworth, and his physical description. Because, if you got the *real* Hyatt Tolman, he's no more a stage robber than you are, or than I am.'

Hale went to the door, opened it and walked out into the shadows. Behind him,

Sheriff Morse closed the door, shot Hyatt an uneasy look, returned to his desk and re-seated himself. He picked up Tolman's sixshooter, closely examined it, lay it aside and swung around.

'Are you *that* Hyatt Tolman?' he asked, his voice full of doubt and suspicion.

Hyatt nodded. 'You got any tobacco on you, Sheriff?' he asked.

Tom had some and handed it over. He kept watching Tolman and he also kept scowling, but then, Tom Morse had been a peace officer a long time—since the end of the war in fact—and he rarely believed anything he heard, and sometimes only half what he saw.

'You could still be the stage robber,' he hopefully said.

Hyatt lit up, exhaled and nodded, his gaze across the room serene and gun-barrel steady. 'I could be, Sheriff. I surely could. But I'm not. I told you the gospel truth. I came on to that shack, helped that girl have her pup, and your men walked in an' took me flat-footed.' Tolman brought up the cigarette, took another long drag off it without removing his eyes from Morse. 'And there's just one more thing to tell: When Sim and his friends took me, they didn't look any further.'

'Meaning?'

'Meaning that about a hundred feet south of that shack was a horse-shed and a little faggot-corral hidden in the live-oaks, where some feller had kept a horse, and where he'd ridden off not more'n maybe two, three hours before I rode in.'

'An' you figure that feller might've been the robber?'

Hyatt shrugged. He didn't know that; he thought now, after he'd had time for reflection, there had to be a very good reason for that man to abandon his wife at her birthing time, and there was, in his mind, just one reason for a man to act like that—to save his life.

Tom Morse craned around as Sam Hale came back into the gloomy office out of the sooty evening. Sam said, 'Light a lamp, Tom; can't you see it's gettin' dark?'

Morse got up to comply. He wasn't looking so grimly pleased now at all. As the light began growing he said, 'You send your telegram?'

Hale nodded, drifting his gaze on over where Hyatt sat relaxedly smoking. 'I sent it. Should have an answer come daybreak.' He cleared his throat. 'Mister Tolman, I'm plumb curious; 'you mind explainin' why you were put in that Yankee penitentiary up in Kansas?'

Hyatt's gaze towards Sam Hale turned ironic. 'You're not nearly as curious as you are interested in whether my tale will jibe with what you've heard,' he said. 'But that's all right, Ranger. I don't blame you for wanting to be sure I'm Tolman.'

Hale smiled a little apologetically. He'd

been seen through and wouldn't deny it.

'I helped burn the town of Martinsburg while serving as a field-commander under General Jubal Early. Both General Early and I were proscribed by the post-war general amnesty for that. General Early escaped. I did not. The general, incidentally, reached Texas, an' for all I know he's still here—hiding, no doubt, because the Yankees still want him.'

Sam Hale gently shook his head at Hyatt Tolman. 'You're Colonel Tolman all right,' he exclaimed. 'You've been in Fort Leavenworth a long time, Colonel. Jube Early got out of the country; he was down in Mexico for a while. Then he went up to Canada. He's not here in Texas, but he was, Colonel. He sure-'nough *was* in Texas.' Sam turned on Sheriff Morse. 'You don't have any stage-robber, Tom. I'll bet my horse'n saddle on that.'

Morse swore blisteringly, something at which he was especially adept. 'Then we got it all to do over again,' he snarled. 'Sam; you got to lend a hand. By this time that outlaw could be thirty miles away an' I'm just about rode down to a nubbin.'

Hale said, with a hard, small smile, 'Let the colonel help, Tom. I've heard it said by some of the old cavalrymen Colonel Tolman was the toughest disciplinarian, the hardest rider an' the straightest shooter in the whole cussed Secesh army.'

'If he's much of a man,' spoke up Hyatt

29

Tolman, 'he won't be more than thirty miles off, Sheriff. That was his woman I he'ped today. That's his daughter they'll be fetching back to Canebrake. What's left to a man—*if* he's a man—after he's got his saddlebags full of gold, exceptin' his woman and his child?'

Sam Hale, with that same little quirked-up grin, said, 'See, Tom; the colonel's already he'pin' you.'

Tolman dropped his smoke, savagely ground it out underfoot and raised cold, angry eyes to the Ranger. 'Call me that just once more,' he exclaimed, 'and gun or no gun I'll be all over you like a rash.'

Hale wasn't surprised. He didn't seem to even be disturbed, although his grin winked out as he and Hyatt exchanged a long, long look. Then Hale lifted his shoulders and let them fall, pushed back up to his feet and sauntered to the door.

'See you in the mornin',' he said to Sheriff Morse, walked out into the night and closed the door softly behind himself.

Tom Morse flung his hat down hard atop his desk, ran bent fingers through his sweat-curled hair and roared a muted curse. 'It'd have sure been simple if you *had* robbed that danged coach, Mister Tolman, an' for lack of anyone better to lay it on, I reckon I'll just sort of lock you up for the night. Come along; there's a drunk Mex *vaquero* in the cell, but he won't bother you.' As Morse fished for his cell-

30

room key he said absently. 'If he does—if he gets to snorin' or something; there's a dipper an' a bucket of water—douse hell out of him.' Morse found the key and bent to open the door. Hyatt Tolman watched him with amusement in his eyes.

Chapter Four

The day was half gone—it was near nine o'clock in the morning—before Tom Morse brought Hyatt Tolman a tray of fried beans and black coffee, and deliberately left the cell door open. He stood out there in the gloomy little windowless hall dourly considering his prisoner.

'You forgot to lock the door,' said Hyatt, gazing out.

'Naw I didn't,' grumbled Morse. 'When you're finished breakfastin' come on out into the office. Sam Hale's out there.'

Hyatt began to understand why no one had showed up earlier; he also understood Tom Morse's glum look. 'Hale got the answer to his telegram,' Hyatt said, making a statement of it, and Tom nodded, turned on his heel and walked away.

Hyatt ate thoughtfully. He wasn't particularly hungry. That Ranger had cleared him, which of course made him feel good, but two things tugged at his mind. One was the Ranger; he'd acted half respectful, half antagonistic, last night in Sheriff Morse's office. There'd be a good reason for a man to act like that. And the other thing was the girl; before Hyatt left Canebrake he wanted to see how she was coming along. He had no especial reason for this wish, beyond the natural interest he had as a first-time midwife concerned with the welfare of his patient.

He finished the beans and coffee, put aside the tray and sauntered on out of the cell, closed the door upon his lumpy cell-mate, the Mexican cowboy, who hadn't once awakened, and continued on out into Tom Morse's office. The Ranger was sprawled in a chair out there, sipping black java and idly holding a cigarette. He and Sheriff Morse looked up. Morse's expression was still grim, but Hale nodded pleasantly, and hospitably asked if Hyatt would care for a cup of fresh coffee.

Hyatt declined, also with courtesy, walked closer to Morse and accepted the sixshooter the sheriff held out to him butt-first. As he holstered his weapon he said to Hale: 'You must've gotten the answer to your telegram.'

Hale nodded. 'Yeah; about an hour back. There's one more question you could answer for me, Mister Tolman. Before you fellers burnt Martinsburg, did Gen'l Early put a ransom demand on the town?'

'He did.'

'Did anyone try to talk him out of that, Mister Tolman?'

'Yes.'

'Who was that, Mister Tolman?'

'Me,' said Hyatt, and saw the ranger's eyes drift over to meet Tom Morse's gaze. 'Let me make a long guess, Ranger. You were informed in your telegram that only two men knew who it was who tried to talk General Early out of making that demand on the town—the General, and the officer who tried to talk him out of it—so you figured if I knew about it, I'd be Colonel Tolman. Right?'

Hale put aside his coffee cup. 'Right as rain,' he agreed. 'It was in the transcript of your trial, Colonel. My boss at Ranger Headquarters was judge-advocate; he remembered that and told me about it in the wire.'

'And now you're plumb satisfied who I am.'

'Yes,' stated Sam Hale, and stood up with a sultry little smile. 'An' now *I'll* tell *you* something, Colonel. I had an uncle an' aunt in Martinsburg who got burnt out an' lost everything they had in that fire.'

Hyatt watched Sam Hale; he'd seen this look on the faces of other men since that fiery day. It bothered his conscience now as it had then, and as it also had later, when he'd been tried and convicted for complicity in an act which the law-court had held was not commensurate with the conduct of civilised

33

enemies.

Sheriff Morse cleared his throat, fished around for a tobacco sack and held it out towards Hyatt. 'Have a smoke,' he said clumsily. Then, aside to the Ranger: 'That was a long time ago, Sam. Besides, you were in the same army as the colonel here; the same army I was in too, and most other Texas-boys was in.'

Hyatt took the sack, lowered his head and impassively went to work. Afterwards, lighting up, he handed back the makings and looked at Sam Hale. 'I was against the burning of that town,' he said. 'If your head-ranger was a judge-advocate, he can tell you as much, Ranger. I'm sorry about your uncle an' aunt's place. That doesn't change anything, I know.' Hyatt exhaled. 'But if your memory's good, Ranger, you'll recall the burning of Martinsburg was in retaliation for the Yankees burning the homes of prominent Confederates. I don't offer that as an excuse here any more than I did at my trial; I only offer it as a mitigating circumstance for General Early, who ordered Martinsburg burned. For my own part—you can believe what you wish, Mister Hale.'

'That's enough,' growled Tom Morse, shooting a tough look from beneath his brows at the Ranger. 'It's done and over with, Sam; besides, there's still that gov'ment money to be recovered, an' the man who stoled it.'

Hale nodded slowly, dropping his gaze from Hyatt Tolman. 'I wish you luck,' he said to Sheriff Morse. 'My orders were to get on back up north.'

Hyatt studied Hale. That the Ranger was a hard but fair man was undeniable, for although he bore animosity towards Hyatt for something which had happened many years earlier, he had also convinced Tom Morse that Tolman wasn't any common outlaw.

Even after Hale departed from the office, though, Sheriff Morse persisted in a grumpy scepticism. He said, 'Mister Tolman, the possemen tell me that there shack was so well hidden in its dry-wash that they'd never have found it 'less they'd been able to keep plumb on your tracks. Now tell me a couple of things: How'd you know where the shack was, an' how come Sim Franklin to pick up your tracks near the holdup site on the north stageroad?'

'The shack,' explained Hyatt, 'just happened to be on my route, an' to tell you the truth, I didn't see it either until I was no more than a hundred or so feet from it.'

'And your tracks?'

Hyatt shrugged. He had no answer for that. Perhaps his captors had picked up his sign where two sets of shod-horse marks had parallelled; where one had shown up more plainly than the others. He said as much to Sheriff Morse and watched the sceptical old law-dog heavily incline his head, looking

35

doubtful but agreeable to this suggestion, and right then it occurred to Hyatt Tolman that Tom Morse was stepping out of character; he just wasn't the kind of a man who'd turn a suspected renegade loose on evidence as flimsy as this. Particularly when the whole countryside was evidently up in arms about this particular crime. He stood there smoking and watching Sheriff Morse until someone rolled a set of bony knuckles across the closed roadside door, then walked on in.

It was big, unshaven Simpson Franklin, looking even more used up and trail-rumpled than he'd looked the day before.

Sim's glance drifted to Hyatt's holstered sixgun then on over to Tom Morse as he said, 'Took us all night an' most o' the morning, Tom, but we got the girl an' her chile over at the hotel.'

'How are they?' Hyatt asked.

Sim looked back at that holstered gun again. He obviously wasn't pleased at what that gun meant—that Hyatt had been set free. 'Well; Doc Crump's stayin' with her, an' he's the best sawbones we got.'

'The *only* sawbones we got,' growled Tom Morse.

Sim let that pass. 'Doc says you done right, mister. Said you tied off the cord real good and she'd have more'n likely died if you hadn't come along.'

Hyatt deeply inhaled and exhaled. It was

36

good to know; it strengthened a man's faith in himself to do something risky and entirely out of his field, and have it turn out right. 'I'm glad,' he said.

Sim faced Sheriff Morse again. 'You turned him loose?' he asked.

Morse nodded without lifting his head or mitigating his scowl.

'He ain't the one, Tom?'

'No, Sim. Sam Hale, one of the rangers from up north, cleared him with a telegram.'

'Well I thought them rangers was supposed to *catch* 'em, not turn 'em loose, Tom.'

Morse raised his eyes. 'If he's innocent, he's innocent, an' that's all there is to it,' stated the sheriff, then leaned back in his chair, his expression altering. 'I know how hard you rode, Sim. I appreciate everything you'n the others have done too, don't you ever figure otherwise. But if Tolman isn't our man, why, I reckon that's that. You sure—'nough wouldn't want the law to send an innocent feller to prison, would you?'

Hyatt, studying big Sim Franklin's face, saw a quick, swarthy shadow pass across the cattleman's features; he thought that it had just occurred to Sim how close he'd come to hanging Hyatt back there in that secret canyon. Franklin looked long and hard at the scuffed, dusty floor.

'No,' he murmured. 'Not if he's innocent, Tom. But now what do we do? That outlaw'll be so far away by now we likely couldn't find him if we had a flying machine of some sort.'

'Go home and get some rest,' said the sheriff solicitously. 'I'll take over from here, Sim. We'll get him, don't you ever think otherwise. One thing about the law, it never gives up.'

Franklin looked as though this threadbare axiom didn't sit too well with him, but he turned doorward, nodded at Hyatt and left.

'You can go too, if you're a mind to,' Morse said to Hyatt Tolman. 'Sorry for the inconvenience.'

Hyatt walked out of the jailhouse, halted upon the planking beyond and looked up and down Canebrake's solitary wide roadway where wagons and riders, buggies and people afoot were passing along. It was close to noon and hotter than the hubs of hell. He spotted Sim Franklin and several other dust-caked, sweaty men up near a saloon fiercely arguing. They would, he surmised, be angrily discussing his release from custody. He also surmised that the wisest course would be to leave this town before he was pointed out to other local hot-heads as the probable gunman who'd held up their stage and shot the armed-guard.

He struck out for the liverybarn.

On both sides of Canebrake's main roadway there were the customary wooden awnings extending from storefronts out to the plankwalk's edge, with supporting upright-posts at spaced intervals. All southwestern towns had these overhangs, and even some northwestern towns had them; they were primarily designed to protect people from the furious heat in summertime, and, to a much lesser degree, to protect them from the torrential cloud-bursts too, but they were never altogether satisfactory against deluges because invariably they leaked at every joint. These overhangs were an American import to the Texas country, where the earlier Mexican settlers had been content to build their mud houses with walls two and three feet thick as insulation against the heat—and also against arrows and bullets.

These overhangs offered a fringe benefit too; men sat upon benches supplied by merchants, sometimes just dozing or whittling, but more often talking and eyeing the pretty girls who walked past. Also, as now, they sat in that pleasant shade considering the strangers who strolled along, like Hyatt Tolman, who got almost to the liverybarn passing a number of these quiet but interested men, before one man spoke out to him.

'You'd be Hyatt Tolman,' this man said, bringing Hyatt to a halt. 'I'm Doctor Crump, Mister Tolman. Sit down and rest your legs for a spell, I'd admire to talk to you.'

What Hyatt saw, upon the bench in front of a harness shop, was not a very prepossessing man. For one thing Doctor Crump had the unnaturally reddish-veined cheeks of a drinker; for another thing he was rumpled and slovenly in attire, less than average in height, and had small, faded gunmetal-coloured eyes that didn't look at a man, they stabbed at him. As he hesitated, looking downward, he recalled a surly comment Tom Morse had made—'The *only* sawbones we got,' Tom had muttered disapprovingly.

'It's about the girl, Mister Tolman,' Doctor Crump quietly said. 'Sit down.'

Hyatt sat. Across the road Sim Franklin and those rough men with him were shuffling on into the saloon over there, looking from the rear as though they were sullenly disturbed about something.

'You did a good job, Mister Tolman. You even bathed the baby just right. Tell me— where'd you find the oil you put on the child?'

Hyatt turned a little so he'd be facing Crump. 'In a bottle on a shelf.'

'Gun oil,' stated Crump, searching Tolman's bronzed, calm features. 'How'd you happen to figure newborns should be oiled?'

'Something I heard once, Doctor, in a bivouac. You know how it is; men talk, and sometimes you pick up information that sticks with you.'

Crump nodded his shockle-head; the hair was coarse, nearly white, and hung in heavy curls. He badly needed a haircut although he'd recently shaved, which was some little improvement; some small concession to cleanliness.

Hyatt said, 'What d'you think, Doctor; will she make it?'

'Oh, yes, she'll make it fine. So will the baby, Mister Tolman. It was her lucky day when you walked in. Real lucky, y'see, because not one man in a thousand would've been able to find that shack—unless of course he already knew where it was.'

Hyatt slowly saw the slyness in Crump's old gunmetal eyes, the craftiness down around the doctor's small mouth. It struck him that this was no chance meeting at all; that Doctor Crump had been sitting up near the liverybarn deliberately waiting for him. It also struck him that Doctor Crump wasn't interested in the girl or the baby; he was interested in that stolen money.

Hyatt got up. 'Nice talking to you,' he said, and walked away. All the way up to the liverybarn he felt those sly old eyes boring into his back.

Chapter Five

He owed the liveryman a dollar, which he paid, and he ignored the rather keen and lively interest the liveryman had for him as he rigged out, stepped up and eased his horse on out into the sunblasted roadway.

He went over to the hitchrack in front of Canebrake's only hotel, swung down and tied up. He hesitated in the shadowy doorway to gaze back across the road. Doctor Crump was still sitting over there, ostensibly dozing in the heat, but Hyatt was not fooled by this. Up at the liverybarn stood the man who'd taken his dollar and had given him his horse. Southward, down in front of the jailhouse, stood Sheriff Morse, his hat tilted, one leg carelessly hooked around his other leg, casually gazing out over his shimmering town. Finally, as he stepped into the hotel's small lobby heading across towards the desk, he met the steady gaze of Ranger Sam Hale. Sam was loafing in a threadbare old red overstuffed chair as though he had all the time in the world. He neither smiled nor nodded as Hyatt strode over to the clerk where he got the girl's room number, then hiked on up the rickety steps.

He halted up there in the murky hallway with its opposing ranks of closed doors, and softly scowled. He'd had his doubts about Tom Morse turning him lose like that; he'd wondered at the ranger's casualness too. Now, it all began to fit a pattern: Morse, Hale, Doctor Crump, even that perspiring liveryman. For different reasons they all wanted to know where the stolen money was hidden, and they all, very probably, thought he might know where it was.

He went along to the fourth room down on the south side, gently rapped, was weakly invited to enter and did so. Someone had thoughtfully pulled the blinds; the room was cool and dark. He made out the sleeping baby in a wicker basket beside the bed. He also saw the girl's wan face turned toward him. She seemed to be struggling to recall him; her gaze was cloudy with uncertainty, as though he seemed familiar to her, and at the same time seemed unfamiliar to her. He removed his hat and tiptoed across to gaze straight downward.

She was pretty. Someone had washed her face and combed her thick, wavy red-golden hair. She was wearing a clean cotton nightdress with little ruffles up around the throat and her hands, lying outside the coverlet, were small and blue-veined. He smiled at her.

'I reckon you don't remember me,' he whispered. 'I was there with you yesterday when the baby came. My name's Hyatt Tolman.'

Her cloudy glance cleared; she made a wan smile showing perfect, small white teeth and a dimple in one cheek. She motioned towards a chair, saying, 'I remember you now. Please sit down.'

'No thanks. I'll be moving along. I just sort of felt that I had an interest in your daughter is all. Just wanted to see how y'all were getting along.'

'Mister Tolman,' she whispered, looking straight up into his eyes. 'They—haven't found him—have they?'

He shook his head. 'It was a foolish thing for him to do,' he murmured to her. 'But the best thing for you is not to talk about it. Not even to think about it.'

Her eyes brightened with quick tears, she clenched her fingers together. 'He . . . there wasn't anything else for him, Mister Tolman. He *had* to.'

Hyatt nodded gently. 'Don't talk about it, even to me.'

'Will—they catch him?'

'I surely doubt it. They wasted a day and a night with me. By now he ought to be clean out of Texas.' He smiled at her. 'Well; almost anyway.'

'Mister Tolman,' she said, turning sober. 'We owe you so much for everything you've done. Curly would thank you if he could, but he can't. Bend lower, Mister Tolman.'

Hyatt bent, thinking she wished to whisper to him. She kissed him squarely on the lips, surprising him, and afterwards she took one of his hands and held it tightly. 'I'll tell Curly when—when we meet again. He'll be very grateful too.'

'Sure,' whispered Hyatt, straightening back up again, freeing his hand. 'Sure he will.' He smiled at her in the cool shadows of the hotel room, grateful she could not see his eyes

44

clearly. He was thinking that she'd probably never see the father of her baby daughter again, and he also bitterly thought it would be better if she never did; a man who would be as plain dumb as her Curly had been, and who had also been as cruel, leaving her like that, wasn't the kind of a man she should ever see again.

'He'll come back, Mister Tolman.'

Hyatt nodded with the bitterness within his heart turning to raw hatred for her Curly. 'You rest easy, Missy. Things'll work out. They always do. And when the baby wakes up, you give her a kiss for me. Do that will you?'

'I'll do it. And I'll never forget you.'

He went to the door, settled his hat atop his head, threw her a last smile and eased quietly out into the empty hallway. He walked as far as the landing and halted. Below him the clerk's balding head shone; over where Sam Hale had been sitting, the chair was empty now.

Curly wasn't coming back, not by his own volition anyway, and probably by now, he'd not be brought back by the law either. What became of a pretty young mother and a baby in a place like Canebrake?

He went downstairs, crossed to the desk-clerk and asked for an envelope. He put seventy-five crumpled dollars inside, sealed the envelope and put it flat down to write her name across it.

He didn't know her name.

The clerk straightened around and looked at him. 'Give this to the girl upstairs with the baby,' he said, handing over the envelope to the clerk.

'Sure enough, mister,' said the clerk, taking the envelope. 'Sure got a tough row to hoe, that little lady, don't she?'

'Tougher than you think, mister,' answered Hyatt, and walked on out to his horse.

Old Doctor Crump was still sitting over there on that bench in front of the harness shop. The liveryman was also still lounging in his doorway across the road. Of Sheriff Morse and the Texas Ranger there was no sign.

Hyatt stepped up across leather and hauled his horse around. Four men suddenly walked out from under the southward overhang ambling into the roadway to block his southward progress. He recognised Sim Franklin first because he was biggest and foremost. Then he also recognised those other three cattlemen as the ones who had been with Sim at the cabin the day before. Hyatt halted, dropped both hands to the saddlehorn and waited. One of those four showed the unmistakable symptoms of whisky. The others, including big Sim, had undoubtedly also been drinking, but they showed it less. Sim Franklin, in fact, seemed as sober as a judge when he spoke up to Hyatt.

'Mister, we been talkin' amongst ourselves,

an' it just don't seem likely you accidental-like come on to that shack. Now I'll sure-'nough grant you had no money pouch on you when we come up, but—'

'Sim,' interrupted Hyatt quietly. 'I don't think you believe I robbed that coach.'

'No?' Growled one of the other cattlemen, blackly scowling. 'Then what reason'd we have fer stoppin' you like this?'

'Wishful thinking,' replied Hyatt, and lifted his reins with his left hand. 'Stolen money, especially if it's hidden close by, has a way of rousing the cupidity of every man around. You're hopin' I know something. But I don't. I never saw the stage, the guard who got shot, the money or the outlaw who took it. Sim . . . ?'

'Yeah.'

'Don't let 'em try for big casino. Not four to one in the middle of the roadway.'

'No one's drawing,' muttered Sim, his squinted eyes turning careful. 'How come it was your tracks that led us to that shack, stranger?'

'It wasn't. Not at first anyway. You picked my tracks up along the way. That's also how you lost the outlaw's sign. But if you really are dead-set on goin' after him, go back to the cabin and ride southward through the trees down there. You'll find a horse-shed with plenty of fresh sign. Trail those tracks, Sim.'

Franklin turned quiet and suddenly thoughtful. The men around him pushed up

47

closer, staring hard at Hyatt. That unsteady one said, 'Hell,' in a scorning tone. 'He's jest tryin' to put us off. I'll show him.' This man dropped his gun-hand straight down.

Sim's breath made a sound as it caught up in his throat. There was the blue-black barrel of a .45 suddenly looking Sim straight in the eye from the right swell of Hyatt Tolman's saddle. Sim hadn't even seen Hyatt's gun-hand move.

'Jamie,' he said huskily to that unsteady cowboy. 'You take your hand off'n that damned gun right now.'

'Why?' complained the drunk man. 'Sim, you said yourself up at the saloon it looked sort of odd to . . .'

'Boy you take your hand off'n that gun!' rapped out big Sim Franklin. 'An' if you think I'm funnin' with you, why you just step up beside me an' look upwards at the stranger's saddle-swell.'

Finally, the others saw that levelled gun. One of them drifted his glance upwards as far as Hyatt's face. This man was suddenly full of grave respect. He said, 'Stranger; you jest ride on if you're a mind to. Maybe it's like you done said—maybe it's that we was *hopin'* more than thinkin'. Boys—Sim—step out of the gent'man's way.'

Hyatt holstered his gun and gently wagged his head at Sim. 'I figured you different,' he said, and eased out southward walking his horse right on past. He didn't turn to look back either, although for some distance, until he was down where the plain and town met, there was a little odd, tickling sensation up between his shoulderblades.

Southward the flow of land merged far out with a brassy mid-day sky that was faded and pale. Westward, the way Hyatt eventually turned, the heat and blaze of dazzling yellow light didn't seem quite too bad. He rode due westward for more than an hour, then decided for no special reason to angle southward a few degrees. He knew from hard experience that due west was at least one secret canyon, and because he had no wish to ride into any more of those oak-choked places, he angled off southward.

Once, where the land rolled along in a gentle trough to where it eventually built up to a low-lying long rib of gravel, he passed around a brushy shoulder, halted, secured his horse and walked back a hundred feet to where that shoulder of land effectively shielded him.

Sure enough, back a long mile and shimmering in the layers of heat, were some horsemen. He couldn't make out their numbers or their identities, but he didn't have to. It could be the lawmen, Doc Crump and perhaps a crony or two such as that sweated liveryman, or it could be Sim Franklin and his pardners.

Hyatt went thoughtfully back to his horse, got aboard and kept on travelling west. He had nothing to hide and if those sceptical fools wished to follow him, he hoped they enjoyed the trip, because California was a long way off, and men might in time, become lonely enough to team up. He smiled.

It never once occurred to him that perhaps his private fate had decreed that not only shouldn't Hyatt Tolman leave Texas, but that he should never even leave Ellis County.

Beyond that rolling hill he saw the tops of live-oaks and redbarks, indicating that on ahead was another of those canyons, only here it was an obvious thing, not at all like that other canyon had been. He played with the notion of going down into it, threading northward until he'd thoroughly confused his trackers, then emerging again. He didn't do this though, despite a strong puckish desire to make those men back there suffer a little. He instead rode southward until he came to the place where that arroyo petered out upon the plain, and started to cross on past it.

A deep-scored set of shod-horse marks shown against the summer-burnt tawny soil, catching his eye first, then also capturing his whole attention. Those tracks had been made by a man riding hard, riding swiftly. Whoever he was, he'd been coming southward down through the tangle of that north-to-south canyon. No man would preferentially ride through a jungle like that; not, at all times, in the middle of a suffocatingly hot summer—unless he had a very good reason.

Hyatt halted, looked back, didn't see hide nor hair of his trailers, looked northward up that shadowy place, and came to the conclusion that this canyon, and the one where the girl had been, were not only parallel to one another, but weren't more than a mile apart. Unless he was very incorrect, he knew exactly whose running-horse tracks those were. Without a second thought he dismounted, swept off his hat and began obliterating all sign of those marks for fifty feet up the canyon, and for a hundred and fifty feet on southward. He then re-mounted, beat dust from his hat, put it back on and eased out westerly again. Until now he'd been sardonic about that sly pursuit back there; let those hungry men think he'd lead them to a cache of government money. Let Sam Hale and Tom Morse eat their hearts out when they discovered that their sly trick of apologetically releasing him in the hope that he might lead them to the cache, proved quite fruitless.

But now he was thinking differently; he knew something those others would give their left arms to know. He knew in which direction the actual outlaw had gone. He also knew, by tracking that gunman, he just might find both the money and the wanted man.

There was, however, one detail to be taken

care of first. He had to shake off those spying riders behind him. But a man who has come to full maturity as a guerilla cavalryman in a brutal war, survives only through craftiness. Hyatt Tolman, General Jubal Early's eyes, knew a dozen ways to get rid of his pursuers. He'd learned every one of those dozen ways under circumstances much more lethal than this situation he was now in, too.

He poked along with the reddening late afternoon sun falling steadily away westward. From time to time he looked back. It was very important now, that his trailers didn't halt back where those tracks had been. They didn't. They kept right on his trail.

Chapter Six

He sat in a clump of scrub-oaks telling himself he was ten kinds of a fool. Those men, especially Morse and that deceptively mild-looking Texas Ranger, were not the kind of men to play games with. He'd already spent long years in a federal prison; the prospect of returning turned him cold to the heart.

Also, he'd long ago decided that Texas should belong to the Texans who loved it, and he was not one of them. The land was harsh, the weather savage, the people more often than not ignorant, feudal and fierce. He'd seen

52

all the trouble and bloodshed a man had ought to be obliged to see in one lifetime. And, finally, he had no real stake here anyway. He had no real stake anywhere, for that matter. But he kept thinking of the cool touch of that nameless girl's lips and of her position in Canebrake. She couldn't be over eighteen years old. She had a baby daughter to care for. Except for the few grubby possessions in that hidden shack—and the seventy-five dollars he'd left for her with the hotel clerk—she had nothing. Moreover, somewhere in this savage land was an outlaw who'd someday try to go back to her. Not, Hyatt bleakly thought, because her Curly loved her, but because *she loved* him. Curly'd know that; he'd return someday to use her.

Behind Hyatt his horse snuffled and shifted its drowsy stance. He looked back, then forward again. It was turning dark and although he sat in a little gloomy bosque of oaks upon a slope and therefore should've been able to see all around, he couldn't in fact see more than a hundred yards. But he hadn't stopped upon that slope to see anyway; he'd stopped up there to listen. The ways of the hunted did not belong exclusively to outlaws, other men under totally different circumstances also had to learn the rules of survival.

But he didn't pick up a solitary sound that meant anything to him; no rattle of shod hooves crossing a dry-wash; no horses blowing their noses, no strong mutter of men in the clear night time air. It seemed as though his pursuers had either turned back or had done as he was doing—sought out a good place to keep a night-long vigil, and were taking their ease.

He let another hour pass. No one was ever injured being very careful, but many a man had died being *in*cautious.

Finally, though, he mounted up and rode down off the slope, satisfied that if those others were out there, they at least were not close enough to divine his purpose or his course.

He rode back the way he'd come, in the general direction of Canebrake, but more southernly. He came ultimately to that canyon where he'd brushed out the tell-tale tracks, then went right on down-country in the direction that hard-riding man had also gone, but a day earlier.

Pursuit of this kind had its advantages; mainly, it being nightfall with a splinter-moon, he'd be very hard to see. By morning of course if the others wished, they could track him, but by morning he'd have an eight-hour start on them too. The other basic advantage was that the man whom he was after not only couldn't spot Hyatt upon his backtrail, he wouldn't have any idea at all that he was being trailed. Obviously, that fleeing outlaw had laid over somewhere southward the day before; probably in the late afternoon and evening. He'd sat somewhere exactly as Hyatt had also done, watching and waiting, and also as with Hyatt, when he'd been perfectly satisfied no one was coming, he'd relaxed a little.

It was a very natural, even necessary thing, for men to relax after a fierce charge, a wild rout, or a hazardous race for freedom; in wartime as in peacetime, those who lived by the gun accepted all the rules of conduct guns carried invariably with them.

For Hyatt Tolman the problem was a simple one. How far would Curly ride; how far could he go on one horse, or, how far had he intended to go before denning up? Where Hyatt was at a disadvantage here was in not knowing how far up the stageroad above Canebrake that coach had been robbed. If he'd possessed that information it would have been relatively easy to surmise the endurance a tough horse would have, and reduce that into southward miles.

But he didn't know where that robbery had taken place so he had to guess.

This posed no immediate problems though; the outlaw certainly would have ridden much farther southward than Hyatt was when he halted, finally, to rest his animal and to also take stock of his surroundings. There was no one following him, he was satisfied about that. What little light came from heaven was ghostly and weak. He'd covered a possible eight or nine miles and it was still some little time before midnight.

The landforms were changing; instead of the usual west-Texas lifts and swales, tree-dotted and occasionally brushed-over, this southward land seemed more brushy, more rocky, and less amenable to the uses of man. It appeared in the ghostly warm night, to be a jumble of broken, twisted and barren country with little water and flaky topsoil.

It was, Hyatt thought, an ideal country for men beyond the law to hide in; no cattlemen or rangers would ride unexpectedly on to a man down here, and if riders came, a fugitive could be reasonably certain they rode with and for the law.

But Curly wouldn't have stopped upon the edge of this dead world; no outlaw on the run would, so Hyatt pressed on, deeper southward until all around him lay the ancient spires and stone-fields that in ages gone some gigantic upheaval had left here in its twisted wake.

Once, he came upon a little meandering creek, totally unexpected in this place. He watered his beast, filled his canteen with fresh water and pushed on again. He was now, he thought, about where Curly might have halted; at least he thought it would be a safe place for a running man to rest, so he sought a little wind-scourged stony hilltop and made his own dry-camp up there in a chaparral field.

There was a little bunch-grass flourishing here and there close underneath the brush where it was protected from summertime's burning heat. Hyatt hobbled his horse, off-saddled and set the animal loose to forage.

He knew which way was east, so he took his solitary blanket and went over to that eastward slope, sat cross-legged there with the blanket across his shoulders, ate a tin of oily sardines —the rangerider's survival kit—and waited.

He sat as an Indian would have sat; comfortable enough so that he wouldn't have to move after dawn-light came and thereby draw attention to himself in this empty, still land, and he waited.

It was a long wait.

Down the far side of his brushy landswell he heard the horse moving through brush. Overhead that anaemic little moon drifted on down the heavens; the stars began to lose their lustre. Over against the broken east a faint long sliver of brightness, softest blue at first, then palest pink, began to dilute the edges of the night.

He sat on, made a smoke and enjoyed it, stubbed it out, dragged the blanket up a little closer about his shoulders; pre-dawn was the coolest time of day, and sitting like that for so long let him feel the faint chill.

When he ultimately moved down off his slope, leaving the blanket behind and taking along his carbine, it wasn't light enough yet to see very far, but what he sought wouldn't be distant anyway.

He'd come straight southward, and that was of course, a gamble; he didn't know that Curly had also ridden down-country in a straight line. Now, he had to course the land for a mile or two, seeking fresh shod-horse tracks.

He did this, also, as an Indian might have done it; he paced along watching the ground, the horizon, and the roundabout places where anyone might be watching. But he angled back and forth, up and down, covering as much country as he could before dawn fully came and sunlight exploded down across this eerie dead world leaving him exposed and noticeable as a moving thing where nothing else moved.

It was a hard search. In fact, with despair mounting in him, Hyatt didn't find those fresh tracks until shortly before the sun's upper curving rim appeared off in the serrated east, and even then, elated though he was, he also was very conscious that he couldn't possibly walk back to his vigil-hill before daylight caught him out there.

He followed those tracks nearly a mile to fix in his mind the direction Curly had been riding, then cut back towards his horse by a deviously circuitous route which allowed him to be sheltered as much as possible by brush.

The sun was a full yard above the earth's farthest rim by the time he got back, rolled his blanket, got his horse, saddled up and led the beast back down through the same underbrush-shield he'd used earlier. He made no move to get astride until he was perfectly satisfied Curly was not close enough to see him—or shoot him. And even after that, he spent another few minutes scouting up his own back-trail. By now his pursuers would be angrily astride, piqued by the way he'd led them a pointless chase the day before, then had struck out down into this unsettled, stony vastness.

But there was no one in sight, northward.

He struck out on Curly's trail again, but distantly parallel, going in close to be sure he was travelling in the right direction from time to time, but otherwise staying well clear for the simple reason that he knew Curly would be watching for just such pursuit. The odds against him finding the outlaw before he was sighted first were not good. He knew that too, but he was making another gamble: Curly, seeing only one man, and a stranger at that who was obviously not a lawman, coming southward, would not shoot unless forced to it. The sound of a gunshot in this empty world could be heard for five miles in any direction. Curly would, if he was a calculating man, and most outlaws were, let Hyatt Tolman ride on past if he could because he would believe it simpler to avoid a meeting than to shoot Hyatt and take a chance on others hearing that shot, coming to investigate it, and perhaps running him down. And not just lawmen either; outlaw-country had more jackals than wolves in it.

As he rode along rummaging the breaks, the boulder-fields, the acres of dense chaparral and sage, Hyatt reviewed his deliberately calculated risks, and finally, for the hundredth time, he deliberated on his reasons for being here. These things always came out the same way, for, basically, a man's initial deductions do not change much; time can and does make alterations in plans, in thoughts, even in intentions, but not enough time had passed yet for this, and therefore Hyatt, being as nature had made him, with his limitations, his margins for error, for sentiment, for risks and for resentment, always came back where he'd started; whatever else Curly was, he had a helpless girl and her child back in Canebrake desperately needing him. Hyatt wasn't concerned with that stage robbery. Even the money Curly had gotten didn't interest him. It was the girl and the baby.

His survival-instinct said time and time again in the dark silence of his mind that none of these people were his concern. But the Hyatt Tolmans of this world are influenced more by conscience than by peril; for that reason, perhaps, they are found in the harsh and lonely places pursuing dangerous dreams.

For as long as the dawn's coolness lingered

it was pleasant riding through this wild country, but as the morning advanced and the heat jelled into an engulfing mass of shimmering pressure, that pleasantness evaporated leaving in its place a dehydrating, de-energising force that leached away all the strength of men and animals. After that happened a man travelled on fortitude alone —'guts' they called it in Texas.

Hyatt began worrying about water for his horse. For himself, he had the full canteen. The land turned even more forbidding too, the farther southward he travelled. Somewhere off in the dancing west, he knew, lay the Rio Grande, but he also knew that this time of year the 'Grand River' was nothing but a chocolate coloured, sluggish run of thick ooze. Still; it was wet, and if he had to, he'd drop Curly's trail in order to save the horse, and ride west.

It was near noon with an enormous, pale-blazing moulten disc standing directly overhead when Hyatt angled eastward to check the trail again. It wasn't there.

He halted, gazed out and around at the blue-blurred jumble of near-desert for a possible place for a man to be holed up, then turned and rode back until he found what he sought; the place where Curly had abruptly changed course, travelling westward now. This time, as he took the outlaw's trail, he remained upon it; no more angling in and out. If he was seen now heading towards the Rio Grande, it would look very natural. Besides that, though, his horse was beginning to suffer from heat and dehydration.

For six miles he stayed on the trail and for six miles the vista remained monotonously forbidding and barren. Then it began to change subtly, to green up a little, to show an occasional tree, some patches of willowy grass, the tracks of foraging animals such as deer, and, finally, he came across a scummed-over greeny pond of water with cattle and horse tracks in the surrounding mud. He watered his own beast sparingly here, saw where the phantom he was following had done the same, then pushed on in that phantom's same tracks again.

The heat was not less, in this fresher country, but the humidity was greater, indicating that the parched land was mostly behind now. Finally, he rode up atop a low hill and halted in the breathless shade of some red-barks, got down and stepped through to the very edge where he could see without being seen, and got a surprise. Not a mile ahead was a set of bone-grey, warped old buildings; a house, several small sheds, and a long, low adobe barn. There were even more trees down there. There were also several faggot-fences enclosing small green pastures where several cows grazed, a few horses switched their tails in shade, and a band of goats wandered contentedly within the confines of their field, safe from the slab-sided coyotes, foxes and little desert wolves.

There was also a big tawny dog down there; he may or may not have caught Hyatt's scent, but something disturbed him anyway, because he came off the ramshackle porch of the main house, halted stiff-legged and throatily barked.

Chapter Seven

At first the barking dog was the only sign of life around the house, but moments later two lanky men came forth, stood upon the porch looking straight up towards Hyatt's hill, and seemed needlessly alert before they strolled on around the west side of the house. One of them re-appeared moments later with a saddled horse and Hyatt's heart sank. But that rawboned Texan down there didn't mount up and head towards the hill, he instead led the saddled horse on down to the barn and disappeared inside with it.

The distance was too great for Hyatt to see whether that horse had the sweat stains upon his coat occasioned by a long, gruelling ride, but he could tell, from the shuffling gait and the head-hung way the animal went along, that he *had* just come in off a hard ride. That, he told himself, would be Curly's horse, and this ranch in an out-of-the-way corner of these badlands, would have been Curly's destination all along. In fact, the man leading that horse under cover could have been the outlaw himself for all Hyatt knew. He'd never seen Curly nor had him described to him.

But it wasn't Curly who was bothering him now, it was that other lanky man down there, and the question in his mind of just how many other men were in that shack. Of one thing he could be quite sure; those men were armed and willing to shoot. More than likely they were also outlaws.

He returned to his horse in the hot shadows and made a smoke. Should he wait for the pursuit to overtake him? At least he'd have reinforcements, willing or not. Or should he simply await nightfall then move in on his own? The chances were good that Morse, Hale, and perhaps even the raffish Doctor Crump from Canebrake would arrive down here sometime in the afternoon or evening. They'd certainly push straight along on the clear trail Hyatt had left.

He inhaled, exhaled, strolled back to study that goat-ranch again; squatted down in the protective shade and thoughtfully smoked. Why, with a good twenty-four hour lead, had Curly come to this place? He had the money, and he'd had nothing to fear from pursuit, so why had he come here? He'd have to share his plunder with that other man, surely. No renegade ever took kindly to dividing his loot.

The answer, Hyatt thought, lay in the land. This was probably the only place within many miles where outlaws could buy fresh horses, food, and a few days' rest before heading on over to the Rio Grande, beyond which lay Mexico and safety from apprehension or extradition. He killed his smoke; it wasn't much of a mid-day meal but at least tobacco had a way of dulling hunger pains.

That man returned from the barn heading up to the house. Hyatt watched him thoughtfully. As he passed in close to the house he paused to say something to the dog and the beast turned and slunk away; evidently whatever it was the man had said, or the tone in which he'd said it, hadn't struck the dog as complimentary.

That dog, Hyatt thought, just might be his biggest stumbling block. After nightfall, except for the animal's barking, getting in close to the shack shouldn't be too difficult.

He returned to his horse, scanned the back-trail, saw nothing, not even any dust, lay out his full length upon the ground, tipped down his hat and closed his eyes. It had been a trying night and the day before hadn't been much better.

When he awakened the sun was falling swiftly, but in size and ferocity it hadn't changed much. What jolted him full alert was that down on the porch of the shack yonder, four men were idly sitting upon tilted back chairs smoking and evidently desultorily talking. He hadn't anticipated *four* outlaws. Curly, he was prepared to face, and even that second man he'd seen earlier, but *four* gunmen was too much.

He had another tin of sardines—his last—checked his horse and returned to the south slope of his brushy lip of land to watch.

Those men upon the porch had evidently eaten, cared for their stabled horses, and were having their final smoke of the quiet, hot afternoon. They seemed much alike, as near as Hyatt could make them out; tall, lean, sun-blackened and well-armed. This was of course a lawless segment of the border-country where, normally anyway, a small band of men were at a disadvantage. But those four down there looked a long way from being helpless. If a larger band of lawless men rode up, Mexican marauders from across the river, or American renegades, Hyatt thought they would look those four over a long time before picking a fight, for obviously, even from his considerable distance, Hyatt could plainly see that there were no cowards or inexperienced men upon that porch.

One of the men flipped away his smoke, got up and went inside. Moments later he returned with a dented tin dish for the dog, whom he whistled up. The dog ate ravenously and afterwards lifted his head, testing the slight stir of late-day air currents. He turned his head directly towards Hyatt's little hill, and barked. His neck-hair raised up; he stood stiff-legged and growled.

That man who had remained standing after feeding the dog, turned to squint in the direction the dog was looking. He spoke from the corner of his mouth to the other three. Only one of them rocked his chair down off the front wall, got up and also looked eastward, but he did this in a manner that indicated no great interest, to watching Hyatt Tolman. The other two went on with their relaxation.

There was a little exchange between those two lanky men upon the edge of the porch, then one of them sulkily shrugged, stepped off the porch and went hiking down towards the barn. Hyatt drew back into the bushes, uneasiness stirring in him. He deduced that the first outlaw, possibly the leader down there, or the owner of the place, had sent his companion to get a horse, to make a scout up towards Hyatt's hill.

When the need for snap-decisions arises, the only man whose judgement is worthwhile is the one who has already been thinking along appropriate lines; Hyatt's judgement was sound enough. It was based upon two things: How fast the far-away sun was descending, and how long it would take that outlaw to get up near enough Hyatt's hill to find his tracks. He thought the outlaw would get around behind the hill before the sun could sink, darkening the world and hiding his fresh sign. He had no alternative, then, if that happened, other than to reach that outlaw before he could spread any kind of an alarm.

Hyatt waited for the mounted man to appear out of the yonder barn with sweat running under his shirt. He dared not trade shots with that man.

When the rider finally appeared the sun was still a yard off the distant horizon. It was going to be close at that. Hyatt let the rider move slowly away from the shack, gratified that the man felt no urge to get on with his scouting, and he finally slipped back away from his position atop the westward slope, returned to his tethered animal, hauled out his booted carbine and went cautiously on down the eastward side of his hill, down into the brush where his tracks were visible leading upwards past the place where he crouched.

Shadows began to thicken on the far side of his hill; visibility was not yet impaired though, and estimating the course, the speed and the probable alertness of the scout, he thought the man must certainly come poking around his hill from the north, before the gloominess thickened enough to conceal his tracks.

That's what happened. The scout came ambling along, riding all loose and easy, not too vigilant but still a long way from being asleep. He should have, by all logic, ridden right on due eastward, but he didn't. Evidently he had no taste for this chore, meant to simply skirt around the hill, emerge along the southward slope and head on back. Of course, this set his course straight for the tracks leading upwards, which Hyatt had made.

Still, the outlaw didn't see those tracks; he was making a cigarette with both hands, his reins flopping, his horse disinterestedly shambling along, as he came within pistol-range of Hyatt's place of brushy concealment. Then the outlaw's horse suddenly caught some faintly lingering scent of horse-sweat, and perked up its ears, quickened its step, and brought the attention if its rider away from the smoke he was making.

This man was obviously a hardened renegade. Hyatt had a good clear view of him from a distance of less than a hundred feet. The man's features were sharp, bronzed, and iron-hard. His eyes, pale in the dark setting of his face, were quick and searching. In the space of one second he'd changed from being sulkily obedient to sharply, sensitively alert. He reminded Hyatt of a lobo wolf who, with every man's hand against him, had developed all his instincts to their sharpest degree. He let the cigarette paper fall, picked up his reins in his left hand and stiffened up there in the saddle. Any chances Hyatt had ever had of surprising this man, were gone.

The horse looked down Hyatt's back-trail,

as though the strongest scent came from that direction. He then swung to gaze on up the hill. Hyatt could have cheerfully shot that horse then and there because the outlaw halted him, turned to look and to also listen, and Hyatt's only alternative to discovery and capture now was to throw down on the outlaw and fervently hope the gunman did not attempt to draw against his drop.

But the outlaw, as Hyatt was carefully raising his carbine, suddenly swung to the ground, stepped up to the horse's head, and stopped dead-still in his tracks as he saw those tell-tale fresh horse tracks. Hyatt had just a split second left and he used it.

He cocked the carbine. 'Freeze, mister. Don't make a single move.'

The outlaw didn't move except to roll his eyes around in the direction of that command. His lipless slash of a mouth showed the savagery his kind usually possessed, though, and Hyatt thought that if that man could have sighted him in the chaparral, in the thickening southward gloom, he'd have tried to draw against him. But there was nothing for the outlaw to see, to draw against, so he stood out there stiff and as deadly as a coiled rattler.

'Shed the gun,' Hyatt ordered quietly.

'Who are you?' snarled the outlaw. 'Step up where a feller can see you.'

Hyatt didn't move. He had this man pegged as one of those wild ones; they rarely lived past their early twenties, but, even so, killing this one wasn't going to improve his own position, so he stayed put and repeated his earlier command.

'Shed that gun!'

The outlaw was clearly balancing something fateful in his mind. He could of course go for his gun, but with no clear target, only a very loose idea of just where Hyatt was, he'd realise how slight his chances were. He reached down and hauled out his sixshooter, dropped it with a bitter oath, and turned fully towards the slope.

Hyatt rose up, eased off his carbine and stepped several feet forward. The two of them exchanged lethal stares for a moment before Hyatt said, 'What's your name, mister?'

The outlaw made a derisive snort. 'Tom Smith,' he growled. 'Or Jim Jones, or Abraham Lincoln. Take your choice. You ask a silly question, stranger, an' you get a silly answer every time. What're you doin', skulkin' around out here? Where's your badge?'

Hyatt shook his head. 'No badge,' he said, on the spur of the moment. 'As for the skulkin', I followed some fresh tracks over here. Now I've answered a few, so it's your turn. Who's in that shack down yonder and how far's the river from here?'

The outlaw's eyes began to turn crafty and appraising. 'The river,' he said evenly, 'is half a day's ride. Only you can't make it 'thout fresh horses, an' the feller who owns that shack yonder—he sort of deals in horses. High-priced, mind you, but then most fellers headin' this way bound for across the river don't have much time for dickerin'. Put up that damned gun; I'm unarmed now. Anyway, it occurs to me maybe you ain't so much in need of that gun ag'in me as maybe against whoever's lookin' for you.'

'Well now,' said Hyatt, leaning his carbine into a nearby clump of sage, 'you just might know what you're talking about.'

The outlaw slowly, wickedly smiled. 'How long you been watchin' from atop that danged hill, anyway?' he inquired.

Hyatt shrugged. 'Couple of hours, maybe. What difference does it make?'

'None, really, only I been arguin' against keepin' a watchdog, and now it seems like I was plumb wrong. The damned dog's been actin' sort of hostile this afternoon an' evenin'. But I didn't figure it was a man—maybe a bitch-coyote or somethin' harmless up there, but not a man.'

'Those tracks I followed,' said Hyatt. 'Who made 'em?'

The outlaw kept on grinning, but his gaze subtly hardened towards Tolman. 'Mister; don't ask so many questions and you just might make it across the river to safety. Besides, that feller don't mean anythin' to you—unless you're one of them undercover sneaks fer the law.'

'Curious,' stated Hyatt. 'I followed 'em a long ways down into this lousy tailend of nowhere.'

'Why'd you follow 'em?'

'Why not?' exclaimed Hyatt. 'I don't know the land. I figured the other feller might know it. Followin' his tracks wouldn't make me any worse off, an' maybe it just might make me better off.'

The outlaw nodded over this, then he said, 'You hungry? You want a fresh horse?'

'How much?' Tolman asked.

The outlaw's smile broadened and deepened. 'What d'you care, stranger; you got money to pay with or you wouldn't be running.'

Hyatt turned quiet now. He'd played this hand for just about all he could; he had to now make a decision whether to go along with the outlaw and hope he could brazen it out, or not. In either case he was squarely in the best position to be killed he'd ever been in, in his lifetime.

Chapter Eight

Hyatt's judgement was effected by the time of day. It was near evening, full darkness would not come for another couple of hours or more, but meanwhile there would be the shadows, the gloomy crevices, the brush-patch silhouettes to shield a man, and also—always in the back of Hyatt's mind—there would be those grim men following him. By now he surmised they'd be at least out where the shod-horse tracks turned abruptly towards this place.

'Well,' growled the unarmed renegade. 'Spit or close the window, stranger. Come on back with me an' meet the others, or try gettin' to the river on the same horse you got down here on.'

'You,' said Hyatt, hearing the menace in those words, 'sound to me like a man who'd go out of his way to make trouble for a feller if he bypassed your friend's ranch.'

The outlaw's lips lifted in a cold and calculating grin. 'Not just me, stranger. Y'see, the feller who owns that goat-ranch around there, well, he sort of takes it unkindly when fellers like you decline to spend a little money at his place. He sort of feels like he owns this country down here—sort of rules it from his shack. No, mister, it wouldn't be just me who'd go after you, it'd be all the boys down there— an' mounted up on fresh horses too.' The outlaw's grin deepened. His eyes turned cold and imperious. 'You think you could out-run us, mister, all the way to the river?'

'Maybe,' exclaimed Hyatt, making his decisions then and there about what he'd do with this man.

'Not a chance,' contradicted the outlaw. 'Not a chance on this earth, feller. So save yourself some bad trouble—come on back and spend a couple hundred—then go on your way with everyone's blessin'.'

Hyatt's expression turned caustic. 'Sure I will,' he said quietly. 'In a pig's eye.'

'Well then, cowboy, let me tell you what'll happen when you try reachin' the river and get overhauled by us fellers: We'll clean you out lock stock'n barrel. Now which is best—spend a couple hundred or lose everything you got?'

'Suppose I don't have the couple of hundred?'

The outlaw lifted his shoulders and dropped them. 'That'd be too bad, because fellers on the run fit into two categories; successful ones who've stuck up a bank or a stage an' have all the gold they can carry—the real professionals. Or damn' fools who shot some feller over a lousy girl an' are on the run with their pockets empty. This latter kind, stranger—well—they just don't never reach the river. They're amateurs, and down here among the professionals we got no use for the amateurs.'

Hyatt walked down closer to the hard-eyed man. 'Turn around,' he coldly said.

The outlaw's grin winked out. His lethal eyes turned wisely knowing. 'No you don't,' he breathed in a gritty whisper. 'You don't knock *me* over the head, cowboy.'

Hyatt took one more inward step and halted. He was within eight or ten inches of the other man. 'You're forgettin' who's giving the orders,' he said, watching the outlaw narrowly, waiting for the lunge, the curse, the swung fist he anticipated.

The outlaw glared. He was tough and hard and ruthless—with a gun. Now he had no gun; he had only his fists. He didn't move.

'Well,' said Hyatt, still waiting, still ready and willing, despising this man for what he was as he despised all men like him.

But the outlaw, without the comfort of his holstered gun, and with the self-inflicted illusion of his invincibility suffering badly from that lack, simply stood there staring. He obviously was a man who'd done his share of murder; who thought of himself as a gifted person, a superior fighting-man. As Hyatt watched though, the outlaw's fierceness atrophied, his eyes clouded up with indecision, his mouth turned loose with uncertainty, and finally with bitterness and self-loathing. He was not going to accept Hyatt's clear challenge to battle. His gun-supported pride and fierce spirit shrivelled in the face of Hyatt's hard-eyed willingness to fight. He became finally, in his own eyes as well as in the eyes of Hyatt Tolman, exactly what he'd always really been—a small man with all the inhibitions, the fears and frights, of all small men. If he'd never been wholly aware of this before, now he *was* aware of it, and whatever happened here between Hyatt Tolman and him, despite the fact that there were no witnesses to his cravenness, *he* knew, and he would never forget, so he was forever after changed. He would never again be the same man he'd been before, and there was no loathing a man was capable of as searing as self-loathing.

'An even break,' he croaked at Hyatt. 'Let me pick up the gun.'

Hyatt considered. He slowly shook his head. 'Too much noise,' he stated softly. 'But except for that I'd let you pick it up. Only, you wouldn't use it. Not now, mister; not against me, now.'

Hyatt reached forth and turned the outlaw with his left hand. There was no resistance; the man knew what was coming and could no longer help himself. Hyatt brought his sixgun up and down in a chopping, hard arc, struck the renegade down across the skull knocking him senseless. The man fell without a sound, almost as though he welcomed oblivion.

Hyatt put up his gun, gazed at the fallen man, stepped across him, bent and raised the limp carcass to dump it across the saddle, then turn and lead the burdened horse back up atop his hill. It was now too dark for the others to find his tracks. They would of course wonder about their companion's long absence, but perhaps not for a while yet, and meanwhile Hyatt had time on his side, for even though those lawmen and townsmen who were trailing him would be forced by the same darkness to halt for the night, he could summon them easily enough if he wished to, by a beckoning finger of fire from atop his hill.

He had something else in mind first, though, and the success or failure of this plan revolved largely around that big cur down at the shack.

He could not hope to get close to those buildings down there as long as that dog was on guard. His scent was strange and therefore hostile to that animal; the dog would raise cane the moment he caught Hyatt's odour, which would in turn bring out those other three gun-men.

But there was a way to minimise that risk. It wasn't foolproof at all, but it was better than perching atop his hill indefinitely, doing nothing, so he unceremoniously dumped the unconscious outlaw upon the ground, began to systematically strip the man of his shirt, trousers, neckerchief, hat, even his soiled and greasy vest. He removed his own clothing and re-dressed in these odorous things. They were not a good fit; the shirt bound him at the armpits and wouldn't meet across his chest. Still, when he was finished, he could have passed in the darkness as that other man. But it wasn't his appearance he was relying upon— it was his smell. He had to fool that dog. The men inside the shack, he'd consider later. He had in mind an ancient trick for them.

He bound his senseless prisoner, gagged the man with one of his own socks, mounted the outlaw's horse and went back down the hill on the far side. It was dark enough now to limit visibility to a hundred feet, more or less. There would be a moon shortly, but a very poor excuse for one.

He paused to retrieve his carbine from the clump of brush near the hill's eastward meeting with flat country, then turned northward and rode approximately in the same tracks the outlaw had made in coming around to him.

When Hyatt was on around his hill bearing northwestward towards the squatty barn, he saw squares of orange lamplight over where the shack stood. Those other three renegades were comfortably inside now, perhaps playing poker or having a drink; he thought that as long as that dog was quiet over there, the men wouldn't come out, and he was correct.

The night was utterly hushed and breathless. Hyatt could have wished for a little ground-swell breeze from the south to keep his disguised scent away from the dog, but he wasted no time on hoping for anything other than another twenty minutes like the previous twenty minutes had been.

He reached the barn, gingerly dismounted, then froze. Standing over in the barn's gloomy square and doorless opening, was the dog. He was looking straight out at Hyatt without wagging his tail, without making a friendly forward move, but, also, without barking.

For a full minute the man and the mongrel regarded each other. For Hyatt Tolman, this was the crucial test of both his canniness and his disguise. He stepped to his horse's head, flung the reins casually across the tie-rack, turned and boldly headed straight for the doorway. The dog seemed undecided, seemed confused as though his nostrils told him this two-legged critter was—and was not—familiar to him. Hyatt halted, bent a little, and spoke quiet words. The dog stiffened. Hyatt went on speaking in a crooning tone. The dog took a forward step and sniffed. Hyatt reached over very slowly, patted the dog's sloping forehead, scratched his back, then knelt as the beast responded with a little tentative wag of his tail, and scratched the dog's back. The animal's lower jaw dropped, he pushed out his head in pleasure from the scratching and brushed up against Hyatt. The confrontation had been met, and triumph, small though it was, belonged to the man. He spent a precious minute talking to the dog and scratching him. By then of course the dog had determined that Hyatt was not, in fact, who he'd originally thought he was, but by then this was no longer the paramount thing, for the man was kindly and a dog such as this one was hungry for friendship.

80

Hyatt finally raised up, looked back towards the house, saw nothing in that direction to alarm him, turned and headed on inside the barn. The dog went padding right along beside him, tail up and wagging, tongue lolling.

There were six good horses stalled in the barn. They were not pet-raised horses, the kind that thrived on apples and lovepats; these were tough, green-broke, snorty beasts that could run forever and exist on a curse and a cuff. They were the kind of mounts wanted men invariably sought and used. They were also the kind of horses that feared and dreaded men, and once turned loose, would be impossible to catch on foot.

Hyatt released them one at a time, led them out through the back of the barn and set them free. He did not do this so that they would all run off simultaneously, causing hoof-thunder in the night. And after that he and the dog walked out to that horse pasture he'd studied from his hill, found the wire gate, threw it aside and also herded these quieter animals out on to the open plain. Here though, he could not prevent all the horses from rushing through that open gap at once. He prayed they wouldn't stampede, but would, being gentler beasts, simply walk away. They didn't though; they were grassed-up and frisky. As soon as they felt freedom, they kicked up their heels and broke away with loud snorts and hammering hooves. Then the dog barked, excited by the flight of those horses.

Hyatt swung around and sprinted for the horse he'd left by the barn. He'd almost reached it when, up at the house, someone came around the side of the building calling the dog by name.

'Sam. Here Sam, boy. Where are you, Sam? What the hell's goin' on out there? Hey Sam!'

Hyatt flung up the reins, vaulted into the saddle, spun the outlaw-horse and broke away eastward in a plunging run. He heard that man up at the house hail him; thought that the renegade might have glimpsed either his silhouette or a look at the horse he was riding, and thinking it was the outlaw Hyatt had captured held his fire.

Whatever kept that man from shooting back there, Hyatt earnestly hoped it would continue to influence him for a few moments longer, and it did. He got well beyond sixgun range, the darkness swallowed him up, and all those angry, wondering renegades back there could now make out was the sound of his mount's hooves striking down over summer-hardened adobe. Hyatt was hidden in the gloom.

The outlaws of course knew which direction he'd taken, and he considered it probable that they'd try finding him. But on foot, which they now were, those men weren't going to go blundering around in the night very long; lifelong horsemen just didn't possess the perseverence on foot they possessed on horseback.

He swept straight on eastward ignoring his hill, his prisoner up there, and his own tethered horse, and rode for a long two miles before hauling his borrowed horse down to a nervous halt. He dismounted, put his ear to the ground and waited. He didn't expect to hear mounted pursuit, but making certain was good policy.

Finally, raising up, satisfied no one was chasing him, Hyatt drew a long breath, held it, then let it out in a long sigh of relief. Now, all he had to do, he thought, was locate Ranger Hale and Tom Morse from Canebrake, surround that shack and smoke out the remaining three outlaws, among whom was Curly, the stagecoach robber.

In the westward distance there was a muffled gunshot, then another gunshot. After that, silence closed in again.

Hyatt stood still, listening. For a long while he heard nothing, but as he was about to get back astride he picked up a quick, brisk little sound of chaparral brushing over something which was running straight towards him. He whipped back around, dipped downward with his right hand and tilted the blue-black barrel of his gun towards that recurrent sound.

The dog came rushing up, tongue lolling, eyes alight. He halted at sight of Hyatt, sniffed, then vigorously wagged his tail.

Hyatt put up the gun, saying softly, 'Sam?'

The dog bounded on up, sat down in front of Hyatt and licked his hand. His tail was sweeping the earth with strong wags.

Hyatt dropped to one knee, grinned and put forth a hand. Big Sam dropped his head to get his back scratched. He'd re-located his friend, and to a dog accustomed to the curses, the kicks and cuffs of outlaws, this friend was the one two-legged thing he'd been waiting all his life for.

Chapter Nine

Hyatt had to alter his plans slightly. It was no longer plausible to light a fire atop that hill back by the goat-ranch to attract Sheriff Morse and whoever else might be seeking him. For one thing the hill was too close to those wrathful men down there he'd set afoot. For another thing they'd not only find their friend whom Hyatt had left trussed up there, but also it now seemed to Hyatt that it would be better if he could have a little time for explaining before an assault was made upon those three outlaws at the ranch.

Sam trotted along at his side as though they were life-long friends. If a thought ever crossed his mind about the renegades far back he'd deserted, the dog never showed it, never looked back even once.

Hyatt turned more loose and relaxed the farther east he rode; the farther he went, the more remote became any chance that his enemies back there could find him or overtake him. He came swinging along through the sooty darkness able to make out nearby objects such as the occasional man-sized boulders or the trees, but otherwise his view was very restricted. Still though, he had something nearly as good as eyes. Sam suddenly halted, sniffed, and the hair along his back rose up. Hyatt saw that, stopped and swung off quickly to squat and gently hold a hand over Sam's mouth.

The roundabout darkness was quiet.

Hyatt gingerly released Sam's mouth. Sam appeared to understand from this that he was to make no noise. The very tip of his tail vibrated as he began moving cautiously ahead. Hyatt took the horse with him as far as the first convenient hitching place then left it and went along behind Sam with his carbine in hand.

A quarter mile farther along Hyatt finally heard sounds. He was in a jumble of big rocks by then, and somewhere not too far off men were grumbling back and forth. There was no little cooking-fire to guide him, but those occasional rough sentences served almost as well. Sam now permitted Hyatt to glide along even with him, and miracle of miracles, Sam didn't make a sound. He was acting now the same way he'd acted back at that adobe barn when he'd first met Hyatt; alert, vigilant, interested, but not truculent.

Hyatt saw them, ultimately, with the aid of watery moonlight reflecting off the rocks against which they were leaning. Sheriff Tom Morse and that Texas Ranger, Sam Hale. He was expecting more men; Doctor Crump, that liveryman back in Canebrake with the lively interest in Hyatt Tolman, perhaps even Simpson Franklin, the rough cattleman. He held back for several minutes waiting for others to walk up. None did. He looked around for their horses but didn't find them, and finally decided those two lawmen were alone.

'Fellers,' he softly said, and saw Morse and Hale jump as though they'd been stung. 'Fellers; take it easy. It's Hyatt Tolman.'

Hale made a little sceptical snort and said, running his glance here and there in the hushed stillness for a man-shape, 'You run out of water, Tolman; why not keep on headin' for the river?'

Hyatt stepped out where they could see him. Sam bristled and made a soft, rumbling-deep growl. Hale and Morse eyed the big dog.

'Who's your friend?' asked the sheriff dourly. Neither he nor the ranger made any move to reach for their hip-holsters.

Hyatt walked on up, mildly amused at the way those two lawmen kept askance looks upon menacing big Sam. 'He helped me set some outlaws afoot west of here a few miles. His name's Sam.'

Morse put up a hand to stroke his jaw and lifted his eyes. 'Why'd you come back; your friends turn against you over the loot, Tolman?'

Hyatt looked past at Sam Hale. 'That was clever of you, Ranger, being so elaborately sly in getting Morse to turn me loose so I'd lead the pair of you to the stage-coach plunder. The only thing wrong, Hale, was that I was telling the gospel truth—I didn't rob your coach and didn't steal your money.'

'All right,' exclaimed the Ranger quietly. 'I'm ready to accept that, Tolman. But tell me one thing: Why all the trick an' fancy ridin'? You said you were California-bound. Well; in case you lost your way, this route'll take you over into Mexico.'

'I'm following the man who *did* rob that coach.'

'You find him?'

Hyatt inclined his head. 'And some friends of his as well. I've got one of 'em tied up atop a little hill. The horse I rode up here on, belongs to that one. But there are three more at a goat-ranch west of here.'

'Humph!' grunted Tom Morse. 'They won't be there now, if you captured one of 'em, stole their danged dog an' rode off on one of their horses.'

'They'll be there, Sheriff, because I also turned all their riding-stock loose. But they'll be expecting us now, too, and from their looks I'd say they're just about the toughest bunch you've ever locked horns with.'

Morse looked over at Hale, but the ranger kept studying Tolman's face. Finally he said, 'How'd you know where to find this stage robber?'

'Found his tracks when you boys were following me yesterday, waited until night time, then struck out southward. Now let me ask you a question: I saw more than just two men trailing me yesterday. Where are they now?'

Morse growled, 'I sent 'em back. They were Doc Crump an' a couple of other danged idiots from town figuring they might find that hidden money before we did. I told 'em all they'd find, if they got that money, was either your lead in their guts or the law's lead; that either way they were playing a losing game.'

'You should've kept a few of them with you.'

Hale looked up. 'Why? You said there are only three of these outlaws; well, there are three of us. A feller can't expect better odds than that, can he?'

Hyatt didn't answer the question. He'd seen those outlaws; they were fierce, wolf-like men and they evidently knew this country very well. 'I don't know which one of them is the man you want,' he stated. 'But my guess is that the others are wanted men too, so maybe, if we can get them all, it won't make any difference.'

Morse fished around for his tobacco sack, lowered his head and went to work creating a smoke. He afterwards offered Tolman the sack and waited until they could both light up from the same match. Hale, who evidently didn't smoke said he'd go get the horses, and walked away. Tom Morse eyed the tip of his cigarette without speaking for a time. Around them the night lay quiet and balmy, little overhead stars wickedly glittered, and there was that faintly acrid desert-smell to the still atmosphere.

'Tell me something,' Morse finally said. 'What's your concern—the money, or the girl an' her baby?'

'It's not the money, Sheriff.'

'Yeah. I sort of figured as much. In fact I told Sam that.'

'He didn't believe you though. He thought I'd hit that stage even when he was knocking himself out to make you think otherwise.'

'Well,' explained Morse, 'that's his job; bein' sly and cautious. But then he's got his private reasons for sort of dislikin' you anyway—Colonel.'

Hyatt turned quiet. Tom Morse smoked and waited until the ranger returned with two saddled horses, then dropped his smoke and stepped upon it as he turned to take the reins of his animal.

The ranger looked westerly with his head

raised as though to pick up a scent. Hyatt saw this and said, 'It's some little distance off. Follow me back to where I left my animal and I'll take you on in.'

For the first time Sam Hale showed by his expression that all his suspicions of Hyatt Tolman were not dead. 'You walk ahead of us back to your horse, an' after that, you ride ahead of us too.'

Hyatt watched Hale step up across leather, turned without another word and, with Sam trotting at his side, went hiking on back to the spot where he'd left his borrowed horse.

It was probably natural for Sam Hale to feel as he felt, Hyatt reasoned. And yet it was a little annoying; if he'd had an ulterior purpose in approaching those two, he wouldn't have had to walk up on them like he did, which he thought Hale should realise; all he'd had to have done was throw down on those two from out in the darkness, disarm them and do whatever he might have had in mind—if he'd been their enemy. But, bearing Tom Morse's words in mind, concerning Sam's disapproval of him, Hyatt relegated this facet of their meeting to the back of his mind.

When he was mounted again he did as Sam Hale had ordered; stayed ahead of them. He rode along back the way he'd recently come speculating on what the afoot outlaws had been doing during his absence. They would of course know that whoever had run off their horses was an enemy. It was his deduction that they would either, knowing this country as they did, or at least as their leader did, make a run for some close-by different spot to make their stand, or else they would be forted-up down in that shack, waiting for whichever came first, armed enemies or the dawn.

When he could vaguely make out the hill from which he'd kept his earlier vigil, and where he'd left his trouserless prisoner, he halted, let Morse and Hale come up on either side of him, and pointed towards the shadowy little hill.

'My horse is up there tied in the trees. So is that renegade I knocked over the head and tied up.'

Morse considered their surroundings, grunted and swung out of the saddle. 'We'd better go on foot from here,' he said.

Hyatt also dismounted, but as Morse and Hale turned to tie their horses he suggested they should hide the animals. He didn't explain why but the other two understood readily enough. If there were three desperate men cornered on ahead, they would be acutely conscious of the fact that any enemies who attacked them would have come up on horseback, and they would, if they could, try to get those horses perhaps even more than they'd try to kill the men who had ridden them into this empty, tortured country.

The dog stayed close to Hyatt; he seemed

perfectly contented. Sam Hale, finished with his horse and examining his carbine, eyed Sam for a moment, then turned back, rummaged in a saddlebag, brought out a strip of nearly black, rock-like jerky, and tossed it to the dog. Sam snapped up the dried meat, wagged his tail at Sam, but stayed beside Hyatt. Morse saw this and flintily smiled.

'Sam,' he drily said, 'you just learnt a lesson. Folks can't buy friends. They can feed 'em until their bellies burst, but they can't buy loyalties.'

Hale grinned. It was the first show of geniality he'd shown since those three tough men had come together in the perilous night. 'Didn't exactly have that in mind,' he drawled. 'Just figured the critter'd be hungry; never saw a dog in my life that wasn't.'

They walked away from the brush clump concealing their mounts, got almost to the hillside, and halted to listen. The night was totally silent, oppressively silent in fact. Hyatt started on up the hill. He moved from brush to rock to brush clump. He expected nothing but life-long caution made him naturally careful. Morse and the ranger grunted along behind him.

They got into the first fringe of trees atop the knoll and halted again. Then Hyatt stole ahead, gliding over where he'd left his horse and his prisoner.

Neither one was still up there.

When Morse and the ranger came up Hyatt told them what had happened and pointed to the places where his prisoner and his horse had been tied.

'That,' said Tom Morse gruffly, 'changes things. Four of 'em couldn't get away on one horse.'

'No,' agreed Hale, 'but one of them could.' He stepped over to the westerly rim and gazed down through the faint-lighted night. 'I think I can make out some buildings yonder,' he said.

Hyatt went out to him and pointed downward and ahead. 'That one is the house; that's the barn farther back. Those other dark patches are sheds.'

Sheriff Morse walked up, leaned upon his carbine and said, 'It's dark down there, like they're all gone.' Then he lifted the Winchester, settled it into the crook of one arm and said, 'But it'd be dark anyway—even if they're layin' for us.'

Hyatt stood in deep thought saying nothing for a while. When the others stirred impatiently he said, 'It's the horse that worries me. Someone rode it away, I'll bet money on that, and if someone did—where did he go?'

Hale turned to Morse. 'Tom; you know this country down here; are there any other ranches anywhere around?'

Morse grimly shook his head. 'Not on this side of the river there aren't, an' in fact this place here was abandoned the last time I

93

chased anyone this far southwest of town. Used to be a family of Messicans lived here. Raised a few pigs, a mess of goats, and raised about a half acre of squash and gourds an' stuff like that. They never made any trouble but I always had a feelin' they didn't just love the country; always sort of wondered if maybe they weren't spies or suppliers for raidin' bands of horse-thieves up out of Messico.'

Hyatt said, 'Where would one man go on my horse then, if there's no nearby ranch where more horses might be stolen?'

Tom shrugged in answer and kept balefully staring down at those dark and forbidding buildings. 'Dunno,' he muttered. 'Maybe nowhere. Maybe they took their friend back to the shack to get him some pants, an' took your horse down there into the barn. Let's go have a look.'

They started moving downward. Hyatt hadn't gone twenty feet when an uncomfortable thought struck him and he halted. 'Suppose they were eastward,' he said, 'listening for riders to come up so they could steal our horses? They're desperate. With only one animal among the four of them, I'd guess they'd be a lot more concerned with getting re-mounted, than with anything else. In their place, I'd be thinking that way.'

Sam Hale scowled and gazed across at Tom Morse; it was evident Hale found Hyatt's logic sound. Tom cast a long, hard look downward at those buildings, then shrugged and turned back. 'All right,' he muttered. 'Let's go back, get the damned horses an' fetch 'em along with us.'

Chapter Ten

It was a good piece of strategy except for one thing; the idea had come to Hyatt a little late. They were passing down the eastward slope again when Sam Hale, striding along in the lead, suddenly threw up his hand. The dog, fifty feet ahead, had suddenly stopped in that bristly and stiff-legged stance of his, and was softly growling deep in his throat.

Hyatt glided up to the dog and, determining the direction of Sam's point, said in a harsh whisper over his shoulder, 'They're hunting the horses; someone is anyway. I just heard metal strike stone out there, like maybe someone's carbine butt-plate hit a rock. Come on.'

They hastened now, no longer going to great pains to be quiet. Silence had been their prime consideration until now. Being set afoot exactly as Hyatt had set the renegades afoot earlier, became their biggest worry now, not silence.

Sam Hale, hurrying along, suddenly uttered an oath and fell. He'd stumbled over an unseen rock up-thrust. Hyatt caught Sam's arm and hauled him back upright. They went along again, but now Sheriff Tom Morse was in the lead, and it wasn't difficult to see from the way Tom was nearly running, that the prospect of losing his horse down in this godforsaken place was uppermost in his mind.

Tom suddenly grunted, halted and dropped to one knee. Without knowing why the sheriff had done this, but sufficiently alert to peril, both Hyatt Tolman and the Texas Ranger also dropped down. Morse pointed northward through the chaparral; someone was stealthily moving over there. Morse lifted his carbine very carefully and waited for a glimpse of movement. He didn't get that glimpse but back where Hyatt was kneeling, someone called softly, quickly ahead. Hyatt swung to look at Sam Hale. The ranger looked back and shook his head; he hadn't made a sound. Hyatt saw Tom Morse turning around in the direction of that call as Hyatt, closest in, began inching through the chaparral. He thought that whoever had risked that quick, brief call, had either become separated from the other outlaws, or had caught sight of the owners of those onward, hidden horses, and was seeking to warn his companions.

The call did not come again.

Hyatt moved swiftly, twisting left and right as he eased ahead through the underbrush. He had his carbine; used it to protect his face and neck from the spiked limbs of sage and chaparral. He was a hundred feet northward of Hale and Morse when he spotted a small clearing on ahead. There was a man out there in plain sight. He was bent from the middle, twisting off to his left, away from Hyatt, as though he'd heard or seen something. Hyatt speculated; he dared not shoot the man and that little clearing was too naked to rush the man—unless . . .

Hyatt drew two bullets from his shell-belt, lobbed one high overhead and heard it fall through the brush out yonder where that man was intently watching. He heaved the second bullet too, put down his Winchester and got up into a straining crouch. As the second bullet made its little rustling sound across the clearing, Hyatt lunged.

The outlaw didn't hear Hyatt coming until a fraction of a second before Hyatt's hurtling form struck him head-on, but even so this man was keyed-up to explosive instant action and half whipped around, half whipped away. Hyatt's thick shoulder caught the taller, leaner man, upsetting him. As the renegade fell his carbine slid out of his hand.

Hyatt came around in a swooping turn and aimed to dive across his foe, but the outlaw frantically rolled clear. Hyatt fought against falling and turned back again. The outlaw bounded up to his feet breathing hard, his eyes bulging, his mouth wide open without a sound coming out of it. The outlaw dropped his right hand, but he wasn't fast enough. Hyatt's blurry speed gave him the drop. He started to raise up with the outlaw under his gun. Hyatt thought it was all over. He had underestimated the man across from him.

'Go ahead and shoot,' said the outlaw thinly. 'They're all around you, mister; one gunshot and they'll close in on you like a pack of wolves.'

Hyatt balanced that thought in his mind, then he said, 'Shed the gun. If you think I'm alone here, you're mistaken. I said shed the gun!'

The outlaw's hard breathing seemed to momentarily constrict as though, accustomed to thinking fast, to making split-second decisions, he'd decided on what he must do. He drew out the sixshooter, then spun sideways and hurled it straight at his captor. Hyatt ducked swiftly from that hurtling gun and had only time enough to drop his own weapon and throw up both arms as the taller man charged into him, his long arms pumping in and out, his big, fisted hands balled up into punishing mauls.

The outlaw was a savage man and a cruel one. He fought with every dirty trick he knew, his elbows, his knees, his butting-head, used at each opportunity. Hyatt gave ground to gain time. He was no novice at this kind of dog-fighting as rangeriders called fist-brawling, but he'd never been able to get set either, so he kept back-pedalling, kept twisting and weaving to dodge as many of those stunning punches as he could.

The renegade went after Hyatt as though his life and liberty depended upon victory, which, in fact, they did. He grunted with the force of his strikes and his rasping breath was loud in the eerie hush of the surrounding night.

Hyatt stepped aside, once, to let his adversary charge past, but the man didn't do that; he was too crafty at this type of fighting. Hyatt swung clear and jumped away. The outlaw came after him, fists held low and cocked, his head curled up into the curve of a shoulder. Hyatt measured his enemy and found him his equal in everything but weight, and compactness, so he jumped in meaning to use this one advantage. The outlaw, believing himself near triumph, was careless; he let Hyatt rush, aimed a blow, and when Hyatt took it glancingly across his forearm deflecting the strike, the outlaw was half spun around by impetus. Before he could whip around, Hyatt had him; caught the man's shirt and belt, set his legs wide and heaved backwards, throwing his whole body into that violent tug. The outlaw flew in against Hyatt and was instantly caught close in a powerful bear-hug.

The outlaw realised in a split second what had happened. Hyatt had used his weight as leverage, had caught hold of his enemy and now the taller man's greater speed and experience were unlikely to prevail.

Hyatt leaned, lifting the outlaw six inches off the ground. He pushed his face hard against the straining renegade's chest to avoid the wild, chopping fists aimed at him. He locked one fist around the wrist of his opposite arm behind the outlaw, and set himself to the powerfully, constricting straining he was capable of.

The outlaw kicked and whipped left and right. He hammered futilely at Hyatt's exposed head. He arched his back and bowed his shoulders. He attempted to trip Hyatt by entwining one long leg around Hyatt's straining knee.

Hyatt steadily increased the pressure. Put all his power and considerable strength into squeezing. He heard the outlaw's breath break out; heard the man's choking, agonised gasp as his bursting lungs fought for the breath which could not get down inside him. He reared back throwing everything he had into his fiercely straining stricture. The raining blows upon his head, his neck and shoulders turned wild and harmless, turned frantically weak and desperate. Suddenly the outlaw went limp. His arms dropped and his hatless head fell forward. Hyatt released his grip and staggered back. The outlaw fell in a heap, senseless.

It hurt to breathe for a while, the balmy

night air was lacking in all the pure oxygen Hyatt needed now. He dropped to one knee and supported himself by one hand pressing upon the ground. He hung like that sucking in huge amounts of air for fully two minutes, and even when the spinning sensation left his head, he was still weak and limp for another five minutes. But recovery, slow as it was, eventually came.

Hyatt retrieved his weapons and his hat. He wiped his .45 off carefully and checked the cocking mechanism to be certain no grit had gotten into the working parts, holstered the weapon and moved across to pick up the guns of his unconscious adversary. With the sixshooter stuck in his waistband and the Winchester in one hand, he went over and gave the sprawled-out tall renegade an impersonal push. The man was totally relaxed and inert. Hyatt flopped him over to see his face. He didn't know the man. He considered his predicament and lifted his head as Sam Hale walked out into the clearing. Sam didn't say a word, he simply strolled up and stood staring at the outlaw.

'Chet Forster,' Hale grunted. 'I didn't know *he* was back in the country.'

Tom Morse came up too. Tom gazed at the unconscious man then up at Hyatt Tolman. 'Must've been quite a fight,' he opined, and might have had more to say except that Hyatt drew in a mighty breath, exhaled it, and jerked his head.

'The horses,' he said. 'There are still three more of these men somewhere around here. Come along.'

Morse was instantly willing and turned to leave, but Ranger Hale said, 'Wait a second,' and bent over to tug off Forster's boots and socks. He also yanked free Forster's trouser-belt and shell-belt, rolled the outlaw over and bound both his arms behind his back with the belts. Then he stood up and nodded. 'He'll keep for a while, but even if he gets his hands loose, he won't go far without any horse or barefoot.'

They pushed straight eastward now, and wasted no more time. The tied horses were no more than a hundred yards or so onward. That the other outlaws hadn't yet found them was entirely due to the fact that Hyatt had initially insisted on hiding them.

Southward off through the chaparral, Sam barked, halting Hyatt and the lawmen, turning them in this fresh direction. Sam barked twice more and over there somewhere a man's ripped-out furious curse sounded loudly. Hyatt spun off in that direction cocking his carbine. Now, this close to the horses, he was no longer thinking of silence or stealth. He was thinking of stopping the outlaws out there in the underbrush.

Sam's third bark was followed by a quick yelp as though someone had struck out at him or perhaps had aimed a kick in his direction. After that the dog was not heard, but by then Hyatt and his companions knew where at least one more of those renegades was.

Tom Morse caught Hyatt's arm dragging him down to a halt. In a harsh whisper Tom spoke and gestured at the same time. 'Tolman; you bear straight on. Sam, you swing off eastward an' I'll swing off westward. We'll maybe catch 'em between us.'

They split up. Hyatt, pushing along, slowed his pace somewhat to permit the peace officers to keep parallel to his advance. He was bending to shove aside a spiny sage limb when a gunshot erupted red and thunderous not a hundred feet dead ahead. He felt the roiled air as that bullet passed along where his head had been a second before, when he'd still been advancing upright. He dropped as though that slug had clipped him, lay perfectly still until he heard a fluting call of inquiry off on his left somewhere, down in the underbrush in the direction Sam Hale had gone, then began crawling forward again, towards the man who had shot at him.

A second gunshot erupted, but this time it was parallel to Hyatt, and northward, up where Tom Morse was. Someone up there but on southward let off an involuntary sharp squawk of purest astonishment, and Morse fired again, evidently this time shooting towards the sound of that quick, sudden outcry.

The man in front of Hyatt was retreating westward; he was making no attempt to be quiet about this withdrawal either. He'd evidently assumed, from Morse's gunshots, that his enemies were cutting him off to the west, were getting between him and the goat-ranch. Hyatt tried hard to estimate this man's route of withdrawal, settled both elbows upon the ground, aimed a foot ahead of where the invisible outlaw was running, and fired. There was a wild threshing of underbrush up there, then silence. Hyatt didn't think he'd been lucky enough to get his man, but he was confident he'd forced the renegade to go to earth and lie still.

Eastward two gunshots erupted almost simultaneously. There was a long moment of silence, then those two duellists back there both fired again. After that, though, both Sam Hale and his adversary turned chary; they did not fire at each other again.

Hyatt got up into a low crouch, cursed the watery moonlight which prevented him from locating the man he'd driven to earth, and started stalking the renegade. Up where Sheriff Morse was, one solitary gunshot erupted, then a deadly silence settled.

Hyatt stopped advancing. He was well within sixgun range of his enemy, which meant that he also was within killing, hand-gun range.

For fully five minutes there was silence all

around. Hyatt dropped flat and frantically rolled sideways as he heard something moving in behind him. It was Sam, sniffing along the ground on Hyatt's trail. For a moment man and dog stared at each other. Then Sam lifted his tail, tentatively wiggled the tip of it as though glad to have found Hyatt, but also as though he was uncertain of his welcome. Hyatt let his breath out slowly and smiled at the dog. Sam shambled on up and sank down. Hyatt reached forth to pat his head, and somewhere southward, sounding even farther out than the base of Hyatt's hill, a man called sharply to other men.

Hyatt thought this would be the outlaw he'd driven to earth and he was right. He was also correct in his surmise that this renegade's call had been to summon his two remaining friends to join him out there. They would undoubtedly be heading back for the shack, on around Hyatt's hill.

It was all over. It had been a narrow thing, but the outlaws had been chased off, the horses were still safe, and, when Tom Morse and Sam Hale came pushing on up through the chaparral, Hyatt was kneeling there scratching Sam's back. The lawmen were dusty and brush-scratched. Morse dubiously eyed Sam and as he knelt he said drily, 'I don't know whether we owe your cussed dog a vote of thanks or a cuff.'

Hale started re-loading his Winchester. As

he did this he growled, 'They'll be back to the shack in a few minutes. Still, we kept 'em away from the horses, and, maybe even more important, we now know where they are.'

Morse spat and ran the back of a scratched hand across his lips. 'I never liked this Injun way of fightin',' he exclaimed, muttering several colourful oaths. 'I'm a daylight man m'self. Never liked skulkin' around in the lousy sage like a damned lizard.' He looked up at Hale. 'Sam; what'd you do with Forster's boots?'

'Hurled 'em away. Don't worry, he won't find em.'

'I wasn't thinkin' of that. I was thinkin' when he comes around he could maybe prance along barefooted as far as their shack.'

But the ranger shook his head about this. 'He'll be asleep for a long time, from the looks of him. Anyway, let's get those damned horses and go on up a little closer. Then we'll be between him an' his friends. If he's crazy enough to try pussy-footin' in through us . . .' Hale lifted his shoulders and dropped them. He had finished re-loading. His unfinished sentence was eloquent. Texas Ranger Sam Hale was a typical man of his place, his time, and his environment; it wouldn't bother him at all to shoot an unarmed man of Chet Forster's stripe.

Hyatt also re-loaded, then the three of them went trudging down to where they'd hidden

106

their horses, got astride, and started back up around Hyatt's little knoll in the direction of the outlaw ranch. It was now, Hyatt estimated, near midnight. There was a little freshening breath of coolness in the night air; it seemed, also, to have a hint of moisture to it, perhaps wafted this far inland from the Rio Grande.

Chapter Eleven

They came around the northerly side of Hyatt's knoll and halted out of sight of the yonder shack and barn. For a moment the three of them just sat there. Upon the ground beside Hyatt, the dog sat relaxed and gently wagging his tail as though all of this was familiar to him, as though he saw no need for fighting, and yet he remained with Hyatt instead of bounding on ahead towards the shack, which in itself was unusual, but as it would turn out, Sam was an unusual dog.

Sheriff Morse's pale-lighted expression was darkly disapproving. On Hyatt's other side the Texas Ranger appeared not quite so bleak, but just as attentive to what lay ahead of them. Since neither Hale nor Morse made the decision, and because he had no intention of sitting out there any longer, Hyatt reined his horse across in front of Sam Hale and started barnward. He did not, however, go in the way he'd be expected to go, for the elemental reason that he was not yet tired of living. He led the two lawmen back eastward a short distance, then due northward, and finally, when he was far out, he turned sharply and headed straight south until he was within Winchester distance of the barn, and there he simply dismounted, tossed one rein to Sam, and walked off to make a scout.

He was still fifty feet away when he heard a horse stamp inside the barn. He halted, fitting this into what he already knew, and went no further. Those outlaws probably were waiting in the barn, not the house. He based this upon the fact that having been stung once by Hyatt they would be unlikely to give him the same opportunity a second time in the same place.

It was a good deduction, but it was false. He wouldn't know just *how* false for another hour, and meanwhile he returned to his companions, told them what he thought, and went west nearly a half mile before the three of them found a good place to secrete the horses again. After that they began their advance upon the barn.

Because of the darkness it was possible to move more swiftly than otherwise. Moreover, because all brush had been cleared away from the goat-ranch long before, they made no noise as they pushed right on up within sight of the barn. Ordinarily this might have also posed a threat because neither was there one shred

of cover anywhere near the barn or other outbuildings, but this was a dark night.

As they neared the barn's rear, doorless
opening Tom Morse put out a hand to brush
Hyatt with it and cause the three of them to
halt. No one said anything. No one had to.
Each of them could feel the peril closing in
around them. Once committed this time, with
most of the advantage with their enemies, it
was highly improbable that the fight would
break up the way their earlier skirmish with
these same men had done.

Morse finally made that same left and right
gesture he'd made before; Hyatt and Sam
Hale understood it. Sam veered off to the
north and Morse went southward. Hyatt, left
alone facing the rear doorway, permitted his
companions sufficient time to get into the
protective cover of the barn's two sides, then
started onward again. By employing extreme
caution he was able to get right up to the
barn's rear wall and flatten there. There wasn't
a sound anywhere. He pushed his carbine
ahead of him and inched up towards that black
opening. Whoever was in there would be alert,
would be waiting. If it was all three outlaws,
then the fight would undoubtedly end here
and now, probably in a wild blaze of red-
orange gunfire.

He got right on up next to the doorway,
paused to listen again, again heard nothing
and slowly went flat down in the soiled dust

out back.

Around the barn's northward side came a faint rustling sound which instantly diverted Hyatt. He waited for it to be repeated but it never was. He thought perhaps Sam had inadvertently brushed the wall or had come unexpectedly against some unseen obstacle. He could envisage the ranger's lips forming sizzling but unspoken oaths over making that little noise.

Hyatt pushed his head far enough around the ground-level mud-sill to peer inside. Because it was very dark in there, much darker than it was outside, he had to hold this position nearly a full minute before his eyes became adequately accustomed to the interior gloom to allow him to see.

He located the horse at once; it was in a tie-stall and it was grey. This surprised him because his horse was seal-brown. Also, that animal in there was not saddled. It made no sense at all for the outlaws to have this animal tied in there unsaddled. Then the animal moved, stepped back with an experienced movement, left the tie-stall it had been in, ambled to the adjoining stall and walked into that one too.

Hyatt let his breath out in a silent groan. That confounded animal wasn't tied at all. It was obviously one of the tame horses he'd turned loose who, becoming hungry and finding nothing worthwhile out on the range,

110

had come on back to rummage in the stall-mangers inside the barn. Hyatt got up on to one knee; he had been fooled as neatly by that horse as though it had been a trap. He stood up, stepped boldly inside the barn and walked on up towards the horse. The beast lifted its long facc, turned and dubiously eyed Hyatt, turned back and went on with its explorations of the manger. Hyatt went on past, halted at the barn's front entrance and hissed for Morse and Sam Hale. They both appeared around the corners of thick adobe which concealed them, glided on up and followed Hyatt back down through the blackness to where that placidly chewing and quite unconcerned old grey horse stood. He explained what had happened.

Sam went over for a closer look at the animal, came back and gave Hyatt a caustic stare. Tom Morse lowered his carbine, blew out a big breath and shook his head. 'Which is worse,' he wanted to know, 'standin' out there expectin' a bullet in the back any second, or findin' out you been made a fool of by an old grey horse?'

Hyatt didn't answer but the Texas Ranger did. 'I'll take being fooled by a horse any day,' he said.

Hyatt, though, suddenly turned and squinted down the rows of opposing tie-stalls. As he completed this study and turned back he said, 'Maybe that grey did us a favour at that;

where *is* my horse?'

Morse looked down the stalls. So did Sam. What Hyatt had said carried a very clear implication. If his horse wasn't in the barn, then it either had to be up at the house, in one of the other roundabout sheds—or gone.

'Gone,' said Morse. 'I'll bet money on that.'

Hyatt raised his eyebrows. 'Where, Sheriff? Where would one man go? Even if my horse would pack double—which he wouldn't; he'd buck somebody off for even tryin' to ride behind the cantle on him—where would that rider go? You said yourself when we first came up here, there were no other ranches close by.'

Morse scowled and shook his head. 'How the hell would I know,' he growled. 'Maybe they drew straws to see who got away all in one piece.'

'Nope,' stated the ranger. 'Tom; you know their kind betten'n that. Besides, there are now only three of 'em. The other two wouldn't let one man ride off. That would mean one less gun.'

'Anyway,' persisted the stubborn sheriff, 'I'll still give you ten-to-one odds somebody rode that horse out of here.' Morse stepped up towards the faint-lighted yonder yard and motioned around with one hand. 'Where could you hide a saddled horse in them consarned little low-roofed goat sheds, tell me that?'

Hyatt was inclined to agree, but he thought they had now to get up closer to the house and see whether or not, somehow, all three of those outlaws hadn't escaped them. He had no idea how the renegades could have done this, but on the other hand he was not going to underestimate those desperate men either; they had taken one bad shellacking this night, if there was a way for them to avoid taking another they would grab at it. He stepped through into the dust beyond the barn and gazed southward, up towards the back of the house. Morse and Hale walked up beside him. Whatever the ranger might have once felt about Hyatt Tolman, he very clearly no longer distrusted him. He said, also gazing southward, 'If one got away on your horse, Tolman, there will be two very desperate men left in that shack. They've got cover and we haven't. The odds're still in their favour.'

Hyatt walked southward but he angled off to the right where several ramshackle little outbuildings cast stygian shadows and where at least some kind of protective cover was handy should they suddenly need it.

Somewhere eastward a goat bleated and Sam the dog, shambling along, suddenly wheeled with a growl and went bounding away. Sam's abrupt movement made the three stalkers dive into the closest cover, which happened to be a low-roofed chickenhouse where Tom Morse, in the act of straightening up again, banged his head on a rafter of dry, rock-hard locust wood. Tom swore fiercely and rubbed his skull.

Hyatt grinned. Sam grinned back; he also made a grimace. 'Nothing's got us spooked,' he drawled. 'A dog makes a jump and the three of us dang near sprang in one another's arms.'

'That damned dog,' mumbled Morse, still rubbing, 'has been trained on sheep an' goats, or I'm a monkey's uncle. A good sheep-dog, when he hears a woolly bleat like that in the night, dashes out to see what's the trouble.'

Hyatt, who had marvelled at Sam's friendliness, came up with an idea which was correct enough although none of them knew for a fact that it was. 'I'll bet you,' he told the others, 'that Sam originally belonged to the Mexicans who settled this ranch. Outlaws wouldn't have a sheep dog with 'em.'

Morse hunched along until he got back out of that shed, straightened up and re-settled the hat atop his head. He was still disgruntled by that bump. Sam did not return and they glided on up closer to the rear of the shack, not halting again until they were close enough to make out every detail of the building. There was a wooden well-box up there scarcely large enough to conceal three good-sized men, but they made it do. Above where they crouched behind the well-box was a locust-limb cross-arm with an iron pulley attached to it, a frayed old rope, and a bucket. This was the place where those outlaws drew their water.

'All we've got to do,' said Morse

sarcastically, 'is keep 'em away from the well for two, three days, and they'll come walkin' out of there with their tongues hanging out.'

Neither Sam nor Hyatt Tolman commented on this; they both understood Tom's feelings. The sheriff felt that he and his companions were no better off now, up close to the shack, than they'd been back at the barn.

Hyatt raised up and gazed at the back-wall. If there was anyone inside that house he had to know it. Otherwise, if those three men had fled, every moment their pursuers spent behind that well-box was giving them more of a head start. Hyatt ducked low, felt around until he found a small stone, raised up and heaved the thing over against the back-wall. Instantly a crashing explosion and a lashing red race of gunfire erupted from the house and a bullet sang lethally down across the yard. Tom Morse dropped flat, twisted to screw up his face at Hyatt and growl, 'Now you satisfied?'

Hyatt was satisfied all right, but what he wished now to determine was just exactly how many renegades were in there, two or three. If it was three, then he could dismiss the mystery of his missing horse as not being pertinent. But if there were only *two* outlaws in there, then one of them had gone for either more horses—or more guns.

Sam Hale pressed up close and said, 'Listen, you two; I think if I drop back as far as that shed where Tom bumped his noggin, I can slip around westerly and approach the house from the side.'

Hyatt shook his head. 'What good'll that do? We already know they're in the cabin, Ranger.'

Morse turned to agree with Hyatt. 'You stay where you are,' he gruffly ordered. 'It may be crowded back behind this danged well-box, but it's cosy, an' right now, with my back exposed northward, I sort of like lots of company around me.'

Hyatt lifted his carbine, rested it across the edge of the well-box and fired without aiming. Instantly gun-fire from the shack erupted as though the outlaws in their cabin had long been expecting this attack and were both willing and ready to meet it.

As Hyatt dropped back down he said, 'Open up, you two. Shoot at anything. Just make them fire back so's we can figure out how many men are in there.'

Sam squirmed around the westerly side of the box, Sheriff Morse pushed his carbine around the east side. Both of them fired, levered and fired again. As before, tongues of red flame sprang out defiantly as the besieged men shot back. When this deadly flurry was finished and silence returned, Hyatt said, 'Two. Just two men in there.'

Chapter Twelve

Tom Morse wasn't surprised or elated about this. His view of their predicament was eminently practical and hard-nosed. 'All right there's just two of 'em in there. All that means is that one of 'em slipped off on your horse, Tolman. But that doesn't make me feel like jumpin' up and cheerin'. We're pinned down beside a consarned well-box with thick plank walls, but we're still pinned down.'

Sam Hale, evidently feeling pretty much the same way, listened to Sheriff Morse but kept peering around his corner of the well-box at the shack. Hyatt, though, was less ruffled, less directly worried over their present situation. He felt in his heart that whoever had ridden off on his horse had done so, not to escape because the others in the cabin never would have agreed to this or even permitted it, but for some other purpose. The only reason he could imagine was either to get horses from some source Tom Morse did not know of, or else to seek armed aid. In either case, Hyatt Tolman, thinking as he'd learned to think in wartime, concluded that those besieged men inside their shack, had to be killed or captured before the third member of their trio returned.

He pushed his carbine over the well-box and fired into the shack. As before, gunfire slashed

117

right back at him. He could feel those slugs ripping into the heavy planking. There wasn't much danger of bullets going through two solid walls of that iron-like locust-wood, not at least until enough lead had been thrown to perhaps weaken the planking, and that would take a long time. Locust-wood, when green, could be moulded and cut to serve its purpose in either building or in fencing. But once it had dried out, it was impossible to even drive a nail into it. It was one of the variety of woods commonly called 'iron-wood'; it was fittingly named. That well-box, old though it was, couldn't have been shattered by bullets unless direct volleys were fired into it for hours on end, and even then, although it might have been cracked, it couldn't have been shredded as pine or fir or bois d'arc could have been.

Still, as Hale said when he drew back to re-load, 'This here is a Messican stand-off, Tolman. We can't get them and they can't get us.'

But Tom Morse, also squirming around to set his back to the well-box, didn't agree. What he said indicated that Tom had been in this predicament before. 'Who's got some matches? That danged shack'll burn like tinder.'

Hyatt and Sam Hale instantly rummaged their pockets. With the ranger it was a good effort but a waste of time. He didn't smoke and therefore had no reason to carry matches,

118

but Hyatt had some. So did Tom. They then began worrying pieces of shaggy bark off the well-box planking, tied several of the little, sparse bundles of this flaky stuff into small switches, and lighted one by hiding the match-flare beneath three battered hats. The bark was dry and therefore should have ignited right off, but it didn't. Locust-wood burned, but it took a good deal of coaxing to make it do so, and even logs of it in a stove or fireplace, didn't flame out like other woods, it put forth a steady blue, peat-like flame of great heat, but it rarely smoked, never popped as pine and fir did, and could hardly be started without a lot of encouragement.

Sheriff Morse swore at the little switch and blew on it. Hyatt and Sam Hale neither blew nor got irritated; they simply watched and waited, knowing eventually their little fire-brand would flame up, and when it eventually did, Hyatt held it straight down until the fire was briskly burning, then he said, 'Get the hats away.' Morse and Hale moved back, Hyatt flung back his right arm and hurled the little flaming firebrand up and over the well-box's cross-arm in a high arc. The thing was seen from inside the shack before it began dropping over towards the house; someone inside bawled out a warning and tilted a pistol-barrel, snapped off a random shot at the whirling little flare of hot light, and missed. Another gun tried also, but the firebrand fell in close to the rear wall and steadily burned.

Hyatt and Tom Morse feverishly twisted up another of their little firebrands. Sam Hale crouched with a ready match and his shielding hat. Inside the house someone opened up on the well-box in a frantic but futile attempt to disconcert the attackers. The well-box shuddered under impact, the yard echoed and re-echoed with gun-thunder, but those three dirty, dishevelled, grim men worked on until, with another firebrand completed and lighted, they waited for the agonisingly slow-to-catch little snippet of blue flame to strengthen. Then Hyatt hurled this one overhand exactly as he'd also hurled the first one.

Now the outlaws inside their shack tried to aim downward along the back wall with their bullets. They were prevented from successfully doing this by the lethal nearness of their besiegers behind the well-box. Once, when a desperate renegade recklessly pushed his hand and wrist through a hole, Sam Hale splattered a bullet within two inches of the man's wrist, causing his aim to be faulty and also causing him to leave a shred of shirt-sleeve upon a weathered splinter as he yanked his hand back inside.

'Now,' said Tom Morse, when a brief respite in the gunfire permitted him to be heard, 'we wait'.

Hyatt had an unpleasant thought. That shack would, as Tom had observed, burn like dry grass. It would also shoot flames a hundred feet into the black night. If there was anyone watching within twenty miles on a still, bell-clear night like this one was, they'd see that hot white glow. This included the outlaw who had gotten away on Hyatt's horse. It also meant anyone else who might be down in this renegade-country. Hyatt said nothing about this though. He didn't intend to, but neither did he get the chance because a long lick of pale flame suddenly ran up the shack's warped, bone-dry back wall bringing an exclamation of grim pleasure from both Sam and Tom Morse.

The men inside now poured both sixgun and carbine fire into the well-box. It was as though, realising they could not hope to get out of their predicament alive once the night was made bright as day with firelight, they were savagely and desperately bent on eliminating their attackers out in the yard.

Sam gave a grunt and jerked back behind the box. A bullet had struck close enough to his right cheek to spray him in the eyes with dust and tiny gritty pieces of rock-hard soil. He rubbed and grimaced and swore. Tom Morse also sucked back. Those outlaws were not permitting anyone to get off a shot from the well-box. Hyatt, seeing the flames brightening the northward yard, was suddenly struck with a thought. He twisted towards Hale.

'Can you see, Sam?' he demanded swiftly.

121

'Yeah; but that sure stung. What's wrong?'

'We've got to get away from here. When that backwall gets to really burning it'll not only be too hot here, but it'll also light us up as well as *them.*'

Tom Morse, listening close by, nodded agreement and began inching away from the well-box. He hadn't progressed fifteen feet when two gunshots shattered the night. Bullets showered Sheriff Morse with dirt and he profanely sprang back to the well-box again where he turned a jaundiced eye upon Hyatt.

'You're the experienced strategist here,' he said. 'Get us out of here.'

Hyatt looked at the ranger. Hale gazed back; his eyes were red-rimmed and leaking water but he seemed otherwise well enough. 'Pick up your gun,' Hyatt said, then turned towards the house, poked up his carbine and waited until his companions were also ready to fire. 'Shoot 'em empty,' he called. 'Draw them into doing the same; make it good enough they'll think we're going to rush 'em.'

When that deafening burst of gunfire erupted from behind the well-box the forted-up renegades reacted to it exactly as they'd reacted to every other gunshot from Hyatt Tolman, Ranger Hale and Sheriff Morse; they met gunfire with gunfire, firing savagely and fiercely, giving bullet for bullet.

The well-box reverberated from those slamming slugs, and over along the rear of the

122

burning shack slivers of wood broke away as the attackers' lead struck ceaselessly against the cabin. It was a deafening roar; the carbines went empty and men grabbed for their sixshooters. The difference between these two weapons, at least in this context, was that the sixguns had a much deeper, throatier roar than Winchester carbines had, but otherwise, if there was any notable difference to both outlaws and attackers, it was in the ringing inside their heads.

But such a wild exchange could only end one way; as Hyatt had planned. When his .45's hammer dropped with a flat clicking sound upon an expended casing, he holstered the gun, picked up his carbine which was also empty, hung there until Tom Morse, also shot-out, looked up from a gunpowder-flecked face, and Hyatt nodded at him.

'I'll go first,' Hyatt said, putting his lips to the lawman's ear. 'If they don't get me you'll know they're shot-out too. Then you and Sam run like the devil was after you.'

Hyatt waited until one of those guns on ahead ceased firing. He then gathered his legs under him and waited for the second gun to slacken off. It did, moments later, and Hyatt sprang up and bolted for that low-roofed little lambing-shed or whatever it was where Morse had bumped his head. He ran crookedly, broken-field running. Behind him a man's excited shout rose up into the ringing stillness following the wake of all that deafening gunfire, but no shots came. Hyatt flung on around that little shed, dropped instantly down and feverishly bent to plugging fresh loads into the Winchester. He would have preferred his sixshooter for this kind of fighting, but with Colt forty-fives it was first necessary to eject all the spent casings before re-loading, and he didn't feel he had the time for that. With the Winchester carbine, which automatically ejected each used casing as a fresh bullet was levered up into the chamber, he had only to push in fresh shells. He did this, and in his haste dropped two.

That same angry shout rose up over by the house again. Hyatt didn't have his Winchester fully loaded but he had six shells plugged into its tube, so he reacted to that yell by jumping around the side of the shed and firing one round into the back of the house from the hip.

Tom Morse and Sam Hale were both sprinting away from the well-box as rapidly as they could flee. One of the invisible outlaws evidently had done as Hyatt had also done; he hadn't completely finished re-loading, but he poked out his carbine through a slot in the burning back-wall and fired anyway. Sheriff Morse gave a tremendous bound into the air and lit running so fast he passed Ranger Hale in a matter of split seconds. Any other time Hyatt would have been amused by that very near-miss. Now, he raised his carbine, took a long rest using one hand to hold the Winchester steady against the shed's rough siding, and fired. His bullet hit the exposed rifle over there between the banded barrel and the magazine wrenching it violently sideways even as its hidden holder squeezed off his second shot. The bullet ploughed a long, raw furrow down the back-wall and the unseen man, with his arm and shoulder badly wrenched by impact, dropped the carbine. It was just as well because the carbine's barrel was hopelessly torn loose of the magazine; the weapon was no longer usable.

Sam Hale was the last one around behind the flimsy shed. He threw himself flat down back there breathing hard, but unhurt. Tom Morse also dropped down, but Tom was holding to part of his trousers up near the thigh. There was a bullethole through the tough, faded blue cloth from back to front. Tom stared disbelievingly at it.

Hyatt stepped back away from his exposed firing position, looked around and stepped still farther back.

Out across the northward yard white flames were casting great, writhing shadows of light and dark. Gradually, those flames were eating their way up the back wall of the shack. Where a bone-dry set of old locust rafter-ends protruded beneath the two-foot overhang, little blue flames were also beginning to burn steadily. There was no hope of the men inside being able to extinguish that fire. No hope at all. They had a choice of two alternatives: run out the front way where the flames could only indirectly limn them, as yet, or throw down their guns and surrender.

Hyatt, correctly assessing these things, said to Morse and Hale, 'Stay back here. They've got to come out pretty soon now—one way or the other. I'm goin' around front. We'll have them sealed off. Shoot if you have to, otherwise, let's try and take them alive. At least one of them.'

Tom Morse raised up and peered around the corner of the shed. Over at the house there was no gunfire now, but Tom suddenly threw up a hand as though there were. He said, 'Hey, Tolman; wait a minute. Look yonder.'

Hyatt and the Texas Ranger, impelled by the breathlessness in Morse's voice, jumped over to also step around the corner of their shed.

A hundred feet eastward from the ranchyard, a man was staggering along into sight. It was difficult to make him out because of the twisting, leaping, convoluting flames which alternately dimmed things down to a smoky sootiness or brightened them into a painful glare.

'One of 'em run out of the shack,' gasped Sam Hale, and raised his re-loaded carbine. 'He acts like he's hit—or drunk.'

Hyatt recognised that man over there and

threw up an arm to knock aside Sam's Winchester. 'Hold it,' he commanded. He had scarcely said those two words when a blast of fierce gunfire broke out over along the back of the cabin. Tom Morse gasped; that staggering man far out across the eastward yard spun and staggered and stumbled ten feet out into the dazzling brightness, then fell headlong, rolled up on to his stomach and lay as still as death.

'Lord,' breathed Sheriff Morse. 'That's— hell's bells, boys, look there; his arms are lashed behind his back with two belts. That's the one we captured. They killed him by mistake; *they thought he was one of us!*'

Tom had called it exactly as it had happened. Neither Hyatt nor Sam spoke; they stepped back out of sight again and gazed briefly at one another. Hyatt then turned away; went hiking on out through the smoky night to establish his vigil around front.

Chapter Thirteen

Gradually but inexorably the shack burned. The rear wall was crackling fiercely before the sides or the front caught, and the second phase of the conflagration included the dust-dry old sun-blasted roof. Where Hyatt stood around front and off a short distance kneeling in the brush, layers of breathless heat came out in

127

waves. He marvelled that those two outlaws were still in the shack, even granting that only the rear of the place and the roof were hotly burning, he thought it would still be insufferably unpleasant inside, and he was right.

But those renegades had their reasons for not coming out; they were wanted men, capture meant lifelong imprisonment, but even worse than that, they knew very well that whoever was attacking them was also quite capable of killing them.

But the best logic on earth could not compel flesh and blood to withstand indefinitely the terribly increasing heat within that cabin, and Hyatt Tolman knew it, so he knelt out there with his hatbrim tilted far down over his eyes to protect him from the growing glare and heat, and he waited.

Around back a gunshot erupted, distinctly audible over the crackling flames. Hyatt re-gripped his carbine and waited. There was no repetition of that shot, but over at the shack's front door appeared a gunbarrel, pushed out between door and doorjam. Hyatt did nothing. The crack over there widened, the carbine barrel protruded almost to the breech. Hyatt saw a thick hand gripping that gun. He waited.

Now, the roof was a mass of flame which crept hungrily from the back of the house towards the front. Writhing silver brilliance began lighting up the front yard as well as it had long ago lighted up the rear yard. Under the little wooden porch-overhang there still remained some of the dinginess of night time. Evidently that man stealthily opening the door and trying to bait Hyatt into firing so his position would be revealed, thought the vague shadowiness under the overhang was an ally, because he hauled the door all the way back. He stepped up into the opening at the same time the back wall and overhead roof began to creak and groan as though they might fall in. Behind that lanky silhouette over there appeared another man, but this one had obviously had enough. He shoved his partner out of the way with a thick arm and jumped across the little porch to land cat-footedly out in the lighted yard, his carbine low-held in both hands and swinging.

Hyatt did not fire.

The man back in the doorway finally walked on out, his movements slow and deliberate. He halted near his companion and said something. He was not holding his carbine in firing position. In fact, this second man seemed fought-out, unwilling to fight on. Behind those two, pitilessly backgrounded by light, the shack's roof ominously creaked and sagged. A shower of tiny sparks exploded upwards into the roiled night air, the man with the gun swung to look back.

Hyatt whistled through his teeth.

Instantly that desperate outlaw over there

129

swung towards the sound of that whistle, his gun rising. The other man did the wisest thing, standing as he was with fire-light making a perfect target of him, he dropped his Winchester, hooked his hands in his shell-belt, and waited.

Hyatt whistled again. This time the armed renegade placed Hyatt's bush and fired into it. That had been the purpose of both those whistles. It is unpleasant to shoot an unresisting foe. Hyatt dropped his cheek against the warm wood of his carbine stock and gently squeezed the trigger. The outlaw jack-knifed. His hat and carbine were knocked away by the impact of that bullet. The man fell face-down. Above him and to one side, still stood that lanky renegade with both hands hooked in his belt. He gazed dispassionately downward, his obvious thoughts turning contemptuous of a young fool who didn't have sense enough to know when he was whipped, or when he was being baited to his death. The lanky man lifted his head, gazing straight over at Hyatt's bush. He started to slowly walk across the yard. Someone northward shouted at him. The outlaw halted, turned very slowly, and waited until Sheriff Morse and Ranger Hale came up, yanked away his sixgun and gave him an onward shove towards the place where Hyatt Tolman was emerging from the underbrush.

The lanky outlaw was a thin-lipped, blue-eyed man burnt nearly black by endless hot summers. He studied Hyatt with impassive close attention, looking away only when Sam Hale ran out where the prone man was and, using his hat to shield his face from the fiercely burning shack, dragged the other outlaw back where the others stood.

'Waste of time,' said the surviving outlaw grittily, bobbing his head towards the man at Sam's feet. 'I saw him get it, lawman. He's deaden'n a mackerel.'

Sam bent to make certain of this and he afterwards straightened up again. That fierce heat was reaching farther and farther out now. Tom Morse motioned with his carbine for the prisoner to precede him in walking farther away. Sam looked down at the dead outlaw. Hyatt saw that gaze and growled: 'Leave him. Where he is right now it's even hotter.'

They went out a hundred yards, halted, turned and wordlessly watched the roof fall, back there, with a loud, ripping sound accompanied by a spiralling great cloud of sparks. Moments later the rear wall disintegrated also, leaving only two walls, the front of the building, and the overhang roof still standing.

The unarmed surviving outlaw turned his head sideways to consider his captors. He was a very calm, unruffled tall man with pitiless, crafty eyes that put Hyatt in mind of a killer wolf. He'd amply demonstrated his total lack of feeling back there where his companion lay dead. He was, in Hyatt's eyes, the most thoroughly deadly kind of a man—one possessing neither illusions nor softness, and one that was capable of watching a friend die as coolly as though that friend was an animal. This man was fearless, crafty and absolutely merciless. He was the embodiment of evil; a man whose humanising juices had long ago been squeezed out of him.

Sam Hale grounded his carbine and fell to watching the prisoner. Sam also seemed to have come to some definite conclusions about this prisoner.

'Hyatt,' he said, over the roaring of the distant flames, 'just in case—how about searching our friend here?'

Hyatt nodded, handed Tom Morse his Winchester, stepped over and ran his hands up and down the renegade. He found a wicked-bladed Bowie knife in a sewn leather sheath inside the outlaw's right boot, and a small, nickel-plated under-and-over .41 derringer pistol in the other boot. He flung those things aside.

Tom Morse pulled his mouth down, saying, 'Regular walkin' arsenal aren't you, mister? What's your name?'

The renegade looked Tom straight in the eye. He was both contemptuous of Morse and unafraid of him. 'I didn't think you'd ever ask, Sheriff,' he said. 'It's James Booth.'

Sam Hale's eyes opened wide. 'Jim Booth,' he exclaimed. 'Jim Booth.'

The tall outlaw lifted a long, knife-edged upperlip. 'Figured you'd have heard of me,' he said to the ranger. 'Folks usually have.'

Sheriff Morse's pulled-down mouth flattened slightly. 'You're proud of that, aren't you?' he demanded. 'A murderer, a thief, a renegade, an' you're proud of it.'

Booth eyed Tom sardonically but said nothing.

Hyatt reached out to brush the prisoner's forearm, attracting his attention. 'How long've you been down here at this shack?' he asked.

Booth shrugged. 'Couple weeks. That feller you shot over there, he owned the place. He'n I used to ride together up in the Cherokee Strip. Come down to visit with him for a spell. Incidentally, his name was Charley Bruton.'

'Sure,' said Sam Hale. 'That explains the mystery of Charley's disappearance. The rangers have been wondering whatever became of Bruton.'

Booth looked at Sam. 'You a Texas Ranger?' he asked, and when Hale nodded, Booth made that cold smile again. 'Well; if a man's got to be taken, I always say it should be done right.'

'It was done right,' snarled Tom Morse. 'The hanging will be done right too, if that's any consolation to you.'

Booth shrugged again. 'I never had any

illusions about livin' forever, Sheriff, or of dyin' of old age.'

'That other one,' broke in Hyatt. 'The one who rode off on my horse; where did he go?'

Booth shook his head, his ice-blue gaze lingering upon Hyatt. 'Couldn't tell you, mister. He just rode away.'

'You're a liar,' stated Hyatt.

Jim Booth's lingering gaze turned shades darker on Hyatt. His faint smile died away. He ran a glance up and down Hyatt's shorter, thicker frame, and said, 'Big talk, cowboy. Big talk. Just how much guts would you have if this ranger and sheriff wasn't here with us?'

Hyatt drew forth his sixgun, handed it to Tom Morse who already had his Winchester, and said, 'Care to find out?' to Jim Booth.

'No,' stated the outlaw without batting an eye. 'Not like this, cowboy, because no matter who might get knocked silly you'd still win. These fellers are on your side, not my side. No. We'll just let this slide for now.'

Hyatt shook his head at Booth. 'Not unless you tell me where your friend went on my horse.'

Now the outlaw's expression altered slightly, turned interested and curious. 'Your horse?' he said. 'Mister; are you the feller who knocked Curly Tonnahill over the head, tied him up an' took away his danged pants?' Booth's little cruel smile came up again. 'Hell; I figured it had to be at least the whole crew

134

of you.'

Hyatt didn't answer. He kept staring over at Booth, turning that name over and over in his head. Curly Tonnahill. Curly . . . He'd had *her* husband right in the palm of his hand!

Tom Morse cleared his throat and spat. He and Ranger Hale exchanged a look. Tom said, 'Tolman; didn't you know Tonnahill was her husband—the baby's pappy?'

Hyatt hadn't known, of course, so he shook his head. He remembered the cruel eyes, the bloodless lips, the murderous and evil slyness of Curly; he couldn't for the life of him, equate that memory with the recollection of that girl's innocence and loving loyalty. It made him a little sick to his stomach to even think of those two together.

Over where the hundred-foot flames were leaping and twisting, there was a sputtering, creaking roar as the shack's outer walls fell inward sending up a huge cloud of flame and sparks and grey-billowing smoke. Hyatt felt something alongside his lower legs and looked down. It was the dog, his little eyes bright in the eerie glow, his red tongue lolling. The others also saw the animal. Jim Booth said, 'So he made up with you boys, did he. I ought to kick his danged ribs in.'

'Lot of things you ought to have done,' stated bleak-eyed Tom Morse. 'Only it's too late now to start any of them, Booth. But I'm sort of like Tolman here; I want to know

135

where Tonnahill went.'

'Go right on wantin',' growled Booth, starting to turn towards the fire.

Sheriff Morse reached out almost lazily, caught Booth's dirty shirt and wrenched the renegade back around, drew him up close and swore at him. 'You ever heard of that Messican saying—*al paredón*? In case you ain't I'll explain it; it means 'to the wall'. In other words—'

'I know what it means,' grated Booth, giving Morse stare for stare. 'An' if you want to shoot me, hop to it—lawman. But you don't scare me one damned bit. Shoot and be damned to you—to all three of you. *I won't tell you where Curly went!*'

Hyatt saw Sheriff Morse's rugged features go pale. He saw the sheriff's right hand tighten around Hyatt's six-gun. Booth was probably closer to death than he'd ever been before. Hyatt reached across, pried his sixshooter out of Morse's powerful grip, put the thing into its holster, and reached up to push Booth and Morse apart. Sam Hale, too, stepped in. Sam didn't want to have to witness a murder either.

Hyatt said, 'Come on, Morse. Let's go down to the barn, rig out that old grey horse down there for Booth, and go get our own horses.'

Tom came down from his height of wrath stiffly and slowly. 'What about Tonnahill?' he demanded. 'He's the one we came down here to find, dammit all. He's the one who—'

136

'For now,' stated Hyatt. 'We'll have to be content with Booth. Anyway, I've got a bad feeling about this. Let's get going.'

Hale nodded agreement, caught Booth's arm and gave him a rough push southward in the direction of the barn. Tom Morse handed Hyatt his carbine and glared, but he said no more, he simply turned and stamped angrily along with the others. Jim Booth was alive, but he wouldn't have been in another ten seconds.

When they got down to the barn with the dog ambling along behind Hyatt, the grey horse was still rummaging systematically through those tie-stall mangers down there. Sam Hale caught him, rigged him out and thoughtfully put a lariat around the animal's neck. He then handed Booth the reins saying, 'Mount up; an' if you feel real lucky, try spurrin' him and making a run for it.'

Booth got astride, cast Sam Hale a hard look, and waited while the three men on foot cast a final long look up at the fiery ruins where the outlaw cabin had been. Now, even the distant well-box was smoking; it hadn't caught fire yet but the intense heat had reached out that far.

Hyatt led the way out to where they'd left their horses hidden. None of them had much to say as they tightened cinchas, turned their mounts before stepping up, and afterwards got astride. Tom held out his hand to Sam Hale for the lariat. Sam shrugged and tossed it over.

Sam and Hyatt exchanged a glance, their thoughts parallelling: If Jim Booth tried anything, Sheriff Morse would kill him. Booth knew that; knew that his most lethal enemy among his captors was Tom Morse, and regardless of his bravery, it was unlikely that Booth was also a fool. He wouldn't try anything, at least not until his position was much improved.

They started off heading northeastward, putting that blood-red fierce glow back there behind them, and gradually feeling the heat lessen upon their backs.

Chapter Fourteen

They rode for an hour and the only thing said was by Tom Morse.

'Fetching back Jim Booth will set some minds at rest up in the Strip, but the stage company, the gov'ment and the folks around Canebrake aren't goin' to be satisfied with that. It's the other one they want, an' it's the other one we came down here to get.'

Sam Hale shrugged. He was impersonal in this affair. He wasn't even supposed to be gallivanting around the countryside, he was supposed to be on his way northward to ranger headquarters. Moreover, the capture of as notorious an outlaw as James Booth, sat very well with him. Not only would it provide him with the best possible excuse for delaying en route, but it would put another feather in the cap of the famous Texas Rangers.

Hyatt Tolman also remained silent and seemingly indifferent. He rode along with his private thoughts. They were neither pleasant nor pretty. Neither had they anything much to do with the prisoner. He was trying to imagine how a man as patently worthless as Curly Tonnahill was, had ever managed to hoodwink that lovely girl back at the hotel in Canebrake. He just couldn't understand anyone, even a girl as young and obviously inexperienced as she was, being taken in by a man like Tonnahill.

Sam Hale, dropping back to ride stirrup with Hyatt behind Jim Booth, glanced across at Hyatt and said, 'You know, my old pappy used to say the worst judge of men—is women. Does that help your thinkin' any?'

Hyatt's eyes crinkled at their outer corners. Ranger Hale was a likable man after he abandoned his antagonism; even an understanding man. 'Yeah, it helps,' he murmured. 'But I had him in my hands, Sam. I could've just as easily gone back and taken him along with me after I set their horses loose.'

'Sure, but you didn't know it then, Hyatt. You didn't even know who he was. In your boots I'd have acted the same way.' Hale gazed on up where Sheriff Morse was grimly riding along. 'We'll get him. Don't worry about that; in time we get them all.'

Jim Booth, listening to this exchange, twisted in the saddle. 'You'll get him,' he confirmed acidly. 'Only when you do, Ranger, you're goin' to wish to heaven you hadn't.'

Hale scowled. 'What's that mean?' he asked, but the outlaw squared back around in the saddle and turned flintily silent.

For another mile they pushed along without any more talk. Hyatt glanced at Booth from time to time. He also glanced over along the easterly horizon. It was now close to daybreak, or he thought it was—thought it had to be. This had been a long, gruelling night. He was tired, thirsty and hungry. The only pleasant interlude all through it had been the dog; Sam was sturdily trotting alongside of Hyatt's horse occasionally looking up, but otherwise accepting whatever was to come next with all the philosophical trust dogs put in the men they attach themselves to.

Booth said to Tom Morse, 'I'm dry as a bone. If you'll bear west about a mile there's a slow-water creek in some rocks. It'll be warm drinkin' but it'll be wet.'

Morse didn't reply. He didn't even look around, but he altered course a little because he too was thirsty and knew that the horses must also be. With a long ride ahead, and with no chance of beating the fierce mid-summer heat, it would at least mitigate the suffering a

140

little to have enough liquid under one's hide to sweat a little.

'Booth,' said Hyatt conversationally, 'tell me something. Tonnahill robbed that stage north of Canebrake and got clean away. Why the devil did he bother going to the goat-ranch; why didn't he keep on to the river and across it?'

'He needed a fresh horse.'

Hyatt shook his head. He had believed this once but having made that same run southward himself, he didn't believe it now. At least he could find a number of good reasons to doubt it, so he said, 'That doesn't figure, Booth. He had a horse that would have made it over into Mexico with him. Hell; I made the same ride, and my horse would have packed me another half day's ride without caving in.'

Booth twisted to throw Hyatt a cold little smile. 'Maybe so,' he said, 'but I doubt it. Forster—the feller who got shot by mistake back there, patrolled the country between the goat-ranch and the Rio Grande. Now do you understand?'

Sam Hale did. He said, 'Pretty neat racket you boys had set up down there. Either a feller stopped and bought a thirty-dollar horse for a couple hundred, or you fellers ran him to earth before he got to the river.'

Booth shrugged. 'Charley used to say it sure beat workin' for a living.'

'Like a bunch of yellow coyotes,' mumbled

141

Tom Morse, listening to this exchange. 'Fellers like you, Booth, don't deserve a trial.'

Booth shrugged again, his expression saturnine. 'Maybe not, Sheriff, but when there's three upstandin', lawabidin' citizens in the posse that takes one of us fellers, there's not too much risk. Some high-minded cuss always stands out for law'n order.' Booth grinned. 'Sheriff; if it'd been just you, I don't figure I'd have got this far. But then if it'd been just you I wouldn't have surrendered, either.'

They came to the sluggish little creek and got down to let the animals tank up. However, the water was unfit for human consumption. It had a greeny, viscous scum along its oily banks. Booth seemed amused at Tom Morse's chagrin. Tom had his canteen, though, so he only swore a little as he and Hyatt Tolman made a cigarette for breakfast. The distant horizon was turning paler than the up-above sky now, and a fragrant pre-dawn chilliness rode the morning air.

'You boys look like hell,' said the prisoner in a low drawl. 'Unshaven, dirty—and you, Tolman—them clothes don't fit you worth a dang.'

Sam Hale glanced upwards from beneath his tilted hatbrim at the captive. 'Let me give you a little advice, mister; watch your tongue. Maybe it's like you said back a ways. Maybe when there's three men you're a heap safer from a bullet than when there's only one man. But, don't put a lot of money on that bet. Three men can keep a secret a heap betten'n ten men could. Down here in these lousy rocks no one'd find your carcass until there wasn't anythin' left but the bones.'

Booth stood there, un-bound, tall and rangy, looking from Sam to Tom, and on over to Hyatt Tolman. He must have seen something lethal in those three faces because he subsided, stopped teasing, and said matter-of-factly, 'Sure, Ranger, sure. Hey, Sheriff, how about some of that tobacco?'

Morse ignored Booth, turned his back on him and quietly watched the eastern horizon where new-day was faintly breaking.

They rested nearly a half hour beside that greeny creek with its sluggish, oily water, then got back astride and headed northeastward again, in the general direction of Canebrake. They hadn't come more than five or six miles from the goat-ranch. That smoke back there stood straight up into the morning dawn scarcely discernible because it, and the brightening paleness, were nearly the same colour.

Hyatt toyed with the riddle of Curly Tonnahill. He had some dark thoughts about Curly's absence but because there was absolutely nothing to substantiate them with, he kept silent. They'd progressed another mile or two when Jim Booth said, 'You know, boys,

143

Curly didn't have no money on him when he got to the ranch, an' that means he hid the danged stuff somewhere.'

Sam Hale sniffed. 'I can't imagine why he wouldn't feel free an' easy among you and Bruton an' Forster, with that loot, Booth. You don't allow it was because he didn't trust you fellers, do you?'

Booth grinned at Sam. 'My, but you got a suspicious mind,' he chuckled. Then he turned serious. 'What I keep wonderin' is—where did Curly cache that money?'

'Don't worry yourself none about that,' growled Sheriff Morse. 'Where you're goin' they don't use money.'

'Sheriff,' retorted the outlaw. 'You know how much money was rifled from that coach?'

'Of course I know.'

'Then tell me this, Sheriff: Is there enough in Curly's cache to maybe make four fellers well off for a few years?'

Tom turned to stare. So did Sam Hale. Hyatt Tolman, who had already surmised what Booth was thinking, only shook his head at the outlaw. 'You're wasting your breath,' he said. 'We're not interested.'

Booth took some convincing on this score though. 'Never was a man born,' he told Hyatt, 'who didn't dream of havin' a big wad of crisp, green cash in his hands, Tolman. You'n your friends are no exception. Let's say he got twenty thousand. That's five thousand dollars apiece. You know what a man can do with five thousand dollars? Buy a ranch, if he wants one, or a fancy saloon in some town, or even a—'

'Like Tolman said,' ground out Tom Morse, 'you're wastin' your breath. Now shut up, Booth.'

Booth shut up, but he also rode along faintly smiling. He thought he'd planted a seed and this was all he'd meant to do anyway. They were still a full day's ride from Canebrake. An awful lot could happen in a day, sometimes.

The eastern world pinked up. Night time's gloomy shadows still lingered in among the boulders and on the west side of brush patches, but new day was definitely here. A long, violent night had ended, and of all the men involved up to now in the fighting, there were several back at the goat-ranch who were no longer capable of appreciating—if they ever *had* appreciated—the haunting beauty, the depthless silence, the fresh, good fragrance, of another dawn, Nature's promise to Man that life was destined always to be renewed, somewhere, somehow.

Hyatt, riding tiredly along slouched and bone-weary, hungry and dirty, turned once to gaze far back. The tall-standing grey smoke with its soiled-looking oiliness, still rose up back there. He thought it would be visible for thirty or forty miles in this more-or-less flat, semi-desert country; thought that as the

145

daylight became brighter, more contrasting, it would stand out even more. There were bound to be rangeriders up around the Canebrake country who would see, and wonder.

Then he caught sight of something else, totally divorced from the smoke and not so far back either; a streamer of musty dust that lay low along the westward sky coming on from the direction of the goat-ranch. He watched this dust-banner for a long time, his speculations concerning the absence of Curly Tonnahill firming up gradually into solid conviction.

'Tom,' he quietly said, 'Sam. Look yonder.'

All of them, including Booth, halted their horses and gazed back. For half a minute no one spoke. That dust-cloud wasn't made by any one rider; it had evidently spiralled to life very recently too—since daylight had made it possible for horse-tracks to be discerned upon the dusty earth.

'That,' Hyatt exclaimed, straightening around in his saddle, 'gives us the answer about Curly. Sheriff; there *was* something down there, after all.'

Morse grimly inclined his head, never once taking his eyes off that distant, swiftly moving cloud of dun dust. 'Yeah; and Curly got to 'em, so I reckon we know now why he ran the gauntlet, also why Booth's been so cocky. How many men you reckon are in that band, Hyatt?'

Tolman didn't bother guessing. It was obvious from the dust that however many there were, they out-numbered Jim Booth's captors by more than two to one.

Sam Hale swore with deep feeling.

Booth relaxed in his saddle, clasped both hands over the horn and looked around at the three glum, concerned faces about him. 'I don't mind telling you now,' he said in a mild, quiet tone of voice. 'Curly rode to a raider-camp we knew about and fetched 'em back. They picked up the tracks after first light— and—there are at least thirty of them, boys.'

'Messsicans,' growled Tom Morse. 'Messican marauders up over the line to steal horses. Is that it, Booth?'

'Not just horses, Sheriff. Money, cattle, jewellery; horses too, of course. But you know how those fellers work. They'll kill lawmen— especially Texas Rangers—just for the hell of it.' Booth's mirthless but strongly confident grin came up again. 'But I'll make a deal with you: Give me a gun, turn me loose, and I'll head 'em off and keep 'em away until you fellers can make a break for it.'

Morse's eyes, bright blue, turned deadly. His lips flattened. 'I got a better idea,' he murmured. 'We kill you right here an' leave your carcass across the trail. That'll stop 'em for a few minutes too.'

Booth, studying Morse's face, saw that the sheriff meant every word he'd said. Booth's

147

confidence wilted, his smile faded out.

Hyatt turned towards the others. He was figuring their chances. Their horses were leg-weary, they, themselves, were in no better shape. The land ahead was mostly open; there was very little hope that, by fleeing, they could accomplish much more than riding their horses into the ground and being set afoot in a country where the sparse cover would permit the Mexican brigands, led by Tonnahill, to surround them.

'What we need,' he said, 'is a miracle. Come on; sittin' here isn't helping any.'

They swung northward and booted their beasts over into a loose lope, the best gait they could use because, although it was not particularly fast, their tired animals could at least keep it up for an hour or so without actually suffering.

The sun jumped up off in the far-away east. At once the coolness diminished and a foretaste of the heat to come turned the air dry.

Booth rode up beside Tom Morse, who shortened the lead-rope between them and refused to even glance over at his companion. Morse had come to a grisly decision about which he would not speak. Whatever happened down here in this empty, tortured world of strong silence and increasing heat, James Booth was not going to ride off if Tom and his friends weren't able to ride off either.

The rearward dust-banner kept coming. It was a long four miles back. The strengthening sunlight caught particles of mica in it, making them burn with a flickering, dazzling brilliance. The riders, though, seemed to neither advance nor retreat after the fleeing men broke over into a lope, and that at least was encouraging.

Chapter Fifteen

They had to slow to a fast walk as the heat increased. That was when Jim Booth shook his head at Tom Morse and said, 'Not a chance, lawman. You'll never make it. Canebrake's still—'

'You,' interrupted Morse fiercely, 'better keep your damned mouth closed. As for making it—don't cheer about that, either, because if *we* don't, neither do *you!*'

Sam Hale told Hyatt he thought one of them might drop back and, with a lot of luck, empty a few saddles back there, maybe even get Curly Tonnahill himself, which would certainly halt the Mexican brigands and might even give the others a chance to reach Canebrake.

Hyatt disagreed. 'The distance is too great, Sam. Besides that, they'd surely kill whoever dropped back, and when the fight gets to us, we'll need all our guns—not just the two that'll

149

be left.'

Hale straightened in his saddle. He didn't say so but he must have agreed with Tolman because he didn't make that suggestion again.

The sun kept climbing. Now it was hot. But the heat affected them in a way unrelated to their predicament. The three of them had been without food or rest for nearly twenty-four hours. Booth was in no better shape, but with him it was different. He could have stopped right where he was and come out of this in fine shape. The lawmen with Hyatt Tolman couldn't do that. Still, the same heat beat upon all of them, turning them lethargic, turning them sleepy in their saddles. It also slowed the shambling gait of their horses. They had to fight constantly against dozing off as they rocked along.

The country was barren again; rocky, brushy, sandy underfoot and gritty with dust that irritated their reddening eyes. They drank from the canteens but thirst wasn't a problem—not yet anyway. Moreover, the canteen water was tepid and tasted rustily stale. Perhaps the sweating horses would have appreciated it, but they weren't in bad shape for lack of water yet. Not after that earlier halt when they'd filled up.

'They've slowed down,' said Hyatt, squinting backwards. It was true. The dust-banner was still back there, but it was no longer rushing fleetly along as it had been.

'I reckon this heat works for both sides,' muttered Sam Hale. 'Suit me fine if it held us both to a walk. We could keep our lead if we never gained a foot.'

Jim Booth, also gazing rearward from time to time, was the one who pointed something disconcerting out to the others. He pointed westward. 'Take a look at that, boys,' he exulted through cracking lips. 'They're *coyote*, those Mexicans.'

They looked and saw at once what Booth meant. The Mexicans had set a small band of their men to pushing ahead faster than the main body. These four or five riders, probably mounted on the best and sturdiest horses, were trying to get up parallel with Morse and Hale and Hyatt Tolman so that they could either charge them from one side, or perhaps get far enough ahead to halt them with gunfire.

'No problem,' muttered Hyatt, the experienced guerilla cavalryman. 'Tom; angle farther eastward. That'll widen the distance, save our horses, and make our friends out there ride twice as far.'

Morse obediently swung off in the new direction. This would of course put them past Canebrake, if they ever got that far up-country, but the peril they negated was here and now; they could worry about succour from town later.

Booth turned his slitted eyes upon Hyatt.

He was wrathful but he held his tongue. He could realise with no particular effort that now could be a very poor time to speak his angry thoughts. Hyatt smiled at him.

The sun climbed steadily on its east-to-west crossing. It lost all its earlier benign pinkness, all its pleasant soft brightness. Heat rolled up off the ground and pressed steadily downward from the brassy skies. It tormented the horses and irritated the men. If there was any advantage under this punishing force, it probably lay with the pursuing Mexicans who were endowed by nature to bear up better under temperatures above a hundred degrees. But Texans, too, had their fierce stubborness, their deadly determination, so, although the three of them suffered, they did not relinquish their grim resolve.

Tom Morse craned around and grunted. 'They're gainin',' he said, and settled back to spur his horse into a lope again. Like the others with him, Tom knew they could not keep abusing their exhausted animals. Unlike the others though, Sheriff Morse began eyeing the tumbles of boulders for a place suitable to defence by three men against perhaps six times that many enemies, perhaps ten times that many. It was not in the Texas character to consider surrender; there was a very good reason for this too—Mexicans would give Texans no quarter. Down the bloody years they never had given them quarter, even when motivated or led by Mexicans of honour, and those men far back were the deadliest Mexicans of them all—border-jumping marauders.

Hyatt drew down to a walk when his horse repeatedly stumbled. 'It's no use,' he said to Sam, as Hale looked around. 'If their horses are fresher we'd better start thinking of how to out-fox 'em or out-fight 'em. We're not going to be able to out-run 'em.'

Jim Booth put a sardonic look of deadly pleasure upon Tolman. 'You're gettin' smart,' he purred. 'I'll still make that trade with you, boys. My freedom for your lives.'

Hale snorted. 'You couldn't prevent those Mexes from shootin' us full of holes if you wanted to,' he said. 'I only hope they'll think you're one of us, Booth, and make you look like a pin cushion too.'

'Not much chance o' that, Ranger,' stated the cool renegade. 'Curly Tonnahill will tell 'em.'

Tom Morse cut in fiercely to say: 'Forget that kind of talk, Booth, because I figure to save the Messicans the lead. You're goin' to die right along with the rest of us—if we're goin' to die. Just you make up your lousy mind to that!'

Booth turned a thoughtful and speculative glance upon Morse. 'Listen,' he said, 'I know how you feel, but I also happen to know it's not just you in this mess, Sheriff. You want these other fellers to die too?'

'They'll take their chances,' snapped Morse, and twisted fully around to squint rearward where the dancing heat was beginning to make the dust-cloud invisible back there.

For another mile they passed along, slowing down to a walk again, and once, as they came abreast of a spiny brush patch that covered nearly an acre, Hyatt Tolman dismounted, walked over into the brush, was gone from sight for a few minutes then walked back, remounted and wordlessly urged his horse onward. No one said anything about this brief halt until, a half mile onward, Sam Hale made a loud grunt. 'What the devil did you do back there?' he asked Hyatt. 'That looks like smoke.'

It was smoke. Hyatt had deliberately fired that brush. Jim Booth shook his head disdainfully. 'If you figure that'll slow 'em down or burn across their path,' he said, 'you're crazy.'

Tom Morse lifted his bushy brows at Hyatt, silently asking for an explanation. Hyatt gave it. 'I wasn't thinking of the Mexicans or Curly Tonnahill. That smoke, when the fire gets going good, will be seen up on the plains around Canebrake. I told you a couple of hours ago, Sheriff, what we're going to need is a miracle. Well; I'm doing my damndest to get us one. Smoke means fire and fire, this time of year, brings men out like nothing else can.'

154

The flame back there suddenly exploded into a searing, wildly writhing sheet of white heat that pushed upwards several huge puffs of black-oily smoke. In that brush patch were varieties of chaparral, sage, and creosote bush, all grease-woods; they burnt fiercely and they also put out billows of dirty smoke.

Booth gave Hyatt another of his hating glares, but as before whcn he'd been angry, he said nothing at all.

Sam Hale and Tom Morse seemed to take some slight measure of encouragement from Hyatt's scheme. Neither of them said aloud they thought it might aid their predicament, but they obviously felt that it conceivably could help, because now they began scanning the onward country as well as the rearward countryside.

Once, where there was a sheet of thin shade standing alongside the eastern side of a big jumble of boulders, they halted to give their worn-down horses a littlc respite. Here, Tom Morse actually handed Jim Booth his sack of tobacco and the accompanying packet of brown, rice-straw papers.

Tom didn't seem changed in any way and when he offered Booth a light he lit his own smoke first, but now there was a hard sparkle of grim hope in his flashing glance. Behind them where that belching brush patch burnt, the heat was unbearable for a mile in all directions. Finally Tom put into words a fringe benefit which was making him feel good.

'Every lousy rattlesnake within a mile back there'll be roasted up out of his hole. I hope Tonnahill an' his friends ride right up into a herd of 'em.'

Booth, silently studying the rearward, yellow-lightcd, brassy land, said, 'Hate to disappoint you, Sheriff. Look off to the west there. The whole band done come together again out there.' Booth shrugged his wide shoulders. 'You made it hot enough to push 'em off the trail a little ways, but it's goin' to take a sight more'n Injun tricks to stop 'em, which is what you got to do. If you can't stop 'em . . .' Booth flicked ash from his cigarette, put the thing between his lips and took a deep-drawn drag without completing his sentence.

They left their thin shade northward bound once more. The pursuit was now visible, from time to time, where brush and boulders parted to allow a long rearward glimpse of the shimmering land. But because those men were riding in a close-coupled group it was impossible to determine their numbers.

'Enough,' growled Sheriff Morse. 'More'n enough of them. I wish to hell the United States dangblasted army had listened to me a couple of years back when I told 'em the only way we'd ever be able to keep these damned Mexes out of Texas was by strong patrols and a big post down here along the Rio Grande. But no; they said us Texans was always bellyachin' about states rights—so for us to go ahead and exert some states rights.'

Sam Hale scratched the tip of his red nose gingerly. His face was taking on another layer of bronze colouring, but in its initial stages it was red, not tan, and it was also tender. His lips were cracking, as were the lips of the men with him. Running a tongue over heat-cracked lips was the worst possible thing a man could do. Sam undoubtedly knew this, but he licked his lips anyway, until Hyatt handed him a little ball of yellow beeswax. After that Sam quit licking and his lips stopped cracking.

Booth held forth his hand for someone's canteen. Hyatt, with more than half the water he'd started out with, gave the renegade his canteen, and afterwards, as he nodded his thanks and passed the canteen back, Booth said, 'Tolman; you're not a lawman. Why'd you do it; why'd you track Tonnahill down to the goat-ranch and make a fight out of it?'

Hyatt dropped his head to concentrate on fastening the canteen. 'You wouldn't understand,' he muttered.

'Try me,' persisted Booth. 'I'm curious as hell. I thought until a while back it was because you had your eye on Curly's stage loot. But that don't gibe; you wouldn't have brought in these two lawmen if that'd been it.'

Hyatt lifted his head, stared straight across and said, 'Forget it, Booth. It's not important.'

Booth wasn't ready to forget it though and

parted his lips to speak again. Sam Hale snarled at him, cutting across those unspoken words with a fierce harshness. 'Rope it! Get off it, Booth, or I'll knock half your teeth out! Square around there in the saddle, ride along and keep your lousy mouth closed!'

Booth stared at Hale; he seemed more surprised than angered. In the end he did exactly as Sam had ordered him to do; squared around and poked along beside Sheriff Morse, who was gazing ironically over at him. Morse said in a soft murmur: 'The quickest way I know to get a bloody nose is to poke your big long beak where folks are tender.'

They went along another hundred yards and the dog suddenly growled, bringing their attention down to him. He was trotting along behind Hyatt but from time to time he'd halt, hackles up, and lift his lips above his fangs and growl off towards the west.

Hyatt looked downward and whipped out his carbine. The dog finally ceased even trying to keep up. He stopped stiff-legged making that menacing snarl deep in his throat. Hyatt slid to the ground, tossed his reins to Sam and made a motion for silence. He gestured towards Sheriff Morse for the others to keep on riding, then he glided over into the closest brush patch with the dog at his heels, and was at once swallowed up in the gelatin heatwaves over there.

Someone, undoubtedly one of those

pursuing raiders, had pushed his horse to its absolute limit to get parallel with the lawmen and their prisoner. Out of a band of thirty or forty marauders there would certainly be at least one reckless soul capable of doing this. Hyatt knew it and with Sam to point the way, he stealthily crept along in search of that man.

And he saw him. The Mexican, with no idea at all that he'd been anticipated, suddenly rose up a hundred yards away, exposed from the waist up, peering over through heathaze in the direction of the fleeing horsemen. Hyatt, knowing that killer would drop down within seconds, raised his carbine and fired. The Mexican's huge sombrero was knocked off and the man went backwards in a drunken stagger. He caught himself finally, and stared straight over where Hyatt was standing, watching. Those two exchanged a long, long stare, then the Mexican suddenly stiffened, fell forward across a wiry sage plant, and hung there. He was dead.

Hyatt patted his dog and trotted out to where Morse and Sam Hale had halted at the sound of that single gunshot. Without a word he mounted, booted his carbine and made a motion for Morse to lead out again.

Chapter Sixteen

'If you fellers ever had a prayer of a chance against those greasers,' said Jim Booth after Hyatt had re-joined them in riding onward, 'you sure spoilt it now. Killin' that feller cooked your goose sure as the devil.'

Sheriff Morse looked sardonically around. 'Like I've said before, Booth, if we get it, so do you, so maybe you'd better start prayin' we make it.'

A thin cry rang out back in that patch of brush where the dead marauder lay. It was a howl of fury and dismay as though the Mexican who had made the outcry had also been a friend of the renegade Hyatt Tolman had killed.

'It stopped 'em for a little,' muttered the ranger, gazing backwards. 'All the same, they're gaining.'

And they were, for after leaving the place where that raider had died, the pursuit increased its gait, probably out of sheer anger, making it possible for Hyatt and his companions to get a fairly good look backwards.

'At least thirty of them,' growled Sheriff Morse. 'I'd trade half what I own right now for a Gatling gun.'

Hyatt saw Jim Booth turn to also gauge the

distance between where he was and where those Mexicans were. 'How come you fellers at the goat-ranch to know that band of raiders was on the Texas side of the river?' he asked.

Booth slowly turned to consider Hyatt. He was slow in answering but eventually he said, 'We knew they were over because Forster, on one of his westward rides, saw 'em. After you run off our horscs an' we went hikin' around in the dark an' come across Curly up there on that little hill without his pants, we drew straws to see who'd take your horse and head for that raider-camp, talk 'em into lendin' us a hand, and that's about the size of it.'

'Not quite,' said Sheriff Morse bleakly. 'How'd you fellers come to be hangin' so close to that goat-ranch if you felt easy about them Messicans bein' up here?'

'Hell,' growled Booth, 'I didn't say we felt easy. We didn't. Especially Tonnahill. He kept sayin' he didn't dare make a run for the river as long as those greasers were between the ranch and the Rio Grande. They'd have likely killed him just for his lousy horse. All of us were waitin' for that band to go on past so we could make our run for Mexico.'

'Honour among thieves,' snorted Sam Hale.

Booth turned on Sam fiercely. 'Honour among store-keepers,' he rapped out. 'Or among any other kind of men who're out to get a stake. There isn't any an' you danged well know it, too. But if it hadn't been that we

161

was a mite worried about that marauder gang, you'd never have found us at the goat-ranch.'

'Tonnahill took a long chance then,' put in Tom Morse.

Booth nodded. 'He had to; we didn't know how many of you fellers were after us. Even after the fight last night east of the shack we weren't sure. All we knew was that someone was out there after our hides. So we drew straws for Tolman's horse, Curly won, and took the chance on goin' down to the Mex camp between us and the river.'

'Probably told them a flock of big fat lies, too,' muttered Sam Hale bitterly. 'Otherwise why would they buy into your fight, Booth? Probably told 'em we had money.'

Booth shrugged. 'I don't know about that. All I'm sure of is that Curly got 'em to come— and right now that's all I care about too.'

Heat compelled the Mexicans to slacken their pace, though, when they were still a long mile rearward. Still, with the fleeing Texans now in sight, the raiders had all the incentive they needed to push this running fight to its grisly conclusion.

Hyatt set fire to another of those big, isolated patches of brush. This one was upon a slight eminence. There could be no doubt at all but that the men up in the Canebrake country would see it.

Sam Hale's horse began to lag. He used his spurs but they had little or no effect. Sam looked helplessly around. 'Done for,' he muttered, and dismounted, looped one split-rein around the horn, kept the other one in his left hand, and walked along leading the horse. Booth looked at him with a cold smile. Tom Morse shook his head.

'How long you figure you can keep up like that?' he asked.

Sam said waspishly, 'You just keep ridin' along and let me do the worrying.'

Hyatt put a speculative glance backwards. The Mexicans were gaining again, but not as rapidly as they had earlier when they'd closed the distance from something like four miles to one mile. As he straightened back around Hyatt saw Sam eyeing Jim Booth's mount, which was still strong. Which was, in fact, the strongest beast they had, which was odd, because the grey horse was also by far the oldest. Hyatt thought he knew how Hale's thoughts were running, and he sympathised with them: Why should the outlaw ride while the Texas Ranger walked?

That overhead sun burned mercilessly. There wasn't a cloud anywhere in all that very pale sky. Heat boiled up underfoot and came down the land in marching ranks. It was by high noon a physical force to be leaned into.

Hyatt watched Sam finish off his canteen and toss it away. He offered the ranger his canteen, which was still one-third full, but Sam shook his head. 'Give me some more of your

163

beeswax,' he said. 'M'damned mouth keeps cracking.'

Tom Morse suddenly lifted his arm pointing on ahead where a fort-like jumble of grey boulders was. 'That's it,' Morse growled. 'Boys; that's it. We make our stand up there. If the folks in Canebrake saw those fires, we'll maybe make it. But whether we do or not there's not a hell of a lot of point in pushin' on past that rock-field, because as near as I can see for the next couple of miles up ahead, there's not another place for us to fort-up.'

Tom's observation was true. One long look round-about convinced Hyatt and Sam Hale of this. They offered no objection as Morse angled along towards that heap of huge old granite stones left in a jumble hundreds, perhaps thousands, of years before, by one of the unpredictable and deadly flashfloods that had been hitting southwest Texas since the Year One. Even Jim Booth seemed to approve, although he didn't say so.

Tom swung off and walked ahead of his horse to inspect the boulder-field. He hadn't advanced fifty yards before Hale said to Booth, 'Hey, gunman; why don't you make a break for it?'

Booth looked disdainfully downward. 'Why; so you can pot me an' get this horse? You go to hell, Ranger!'

Hyatt also dismounted. Sam, the dog, instantly came on up to push his warm muzzle

164

against the man and gently wag his tail.

Sheriff Morse re-appeared through a dusty pathway between several big rocks and solemnly nodded. 'Lead the horses on in,' he ordered. 'There's a reg'lar little open place back in there.' He turned and led the way. By that time Jim Booth was the only one of them still astride, and even he dismounted as his horse began nosing along into rock-pilcs.

'Might be a rattler in here,' Hale said sarcastically. Booth ignored him and walked on ahead of both Sam and Hyatt Tolman.

It was, surprisingly enough, several degrees cooler inside the natural, granite fortress, than it had been outside it. 'Strange,' said Hyatt, looking at the wall of rocks. 'It should be hotter; those blessed boulders'll be too hot to rest a hand against.'

'Let the horses go,' said Morse, moving over to the south wall of rock. 'We'll take turns watching. It should take Tonnahill a little time to get up here. You two fellers take a nap if you want—rest can make a heap of difference.'

Jim Booth stepped around his grey horse to say, 'Why sleep, boys; in another couple of hours you'll be asleep for all time.'

Before Hyatt or Tom Morse, who was too distant anyway, could intervene, Sam Hale lunged, caught the lanky renegade's shirt and spun Booth towards him, at the same time Hale swung a savage blow from the region of his belt. That fist cracked against Booth's

165

surprised jaw with the sound of brittle wood breaking. Booth's head went so violently backwards his hat flew twenty feet away. Then Booth fell, rolled once and lay perfectly still.

'Had enough of his lip,' growled Sam, flexing his fingers and looking defiantly around. Hyatt looked but had nothing to say. Tom Morse only shrugged.

'He's had it coming ever since we took him,' said Tom. 'Anyway, now we can quit worryin' about whether he's behind one of us or not. All right, Sam; lash his danged arms and legs with his belts and get some rest. I'll take the first watch.' As he finished speaking Morse stepped up on to the first boulder, yanked back his palm with a furious expletive, and blew on it.

Hyatt watched the ranger settle himself for rest. He strolled across to gaze at the bound outlaw, found him conscious but gagged, watched Booth's furious eyes roll up to meet Hyatt's downward look, then he strolled on across where the sheriff was.

Morse had a seat six feet above the ground in the rock pile which offered a full ninety-degree view of the southward country. As Hyatt climbed up and hunkered, Morse made a wide gesture and said, 'See everything from up here, Tolman, even that fire you lit 'way back there.'

Hyatt looked, saw the smoke from that fire just fine, but he saw nothing else. He pulled his head back. 'Wasn't much concerned with the fire, Sheriff. Where is Tonnahill and his pepper-bellies?'

Morse reached up to tug his hatbrim lower and to afterwards squint southwestward for nearly thirty seconds before he said. 'Yonder,' and lifted his right hand to point out where the furious heat blurred the land with a grey haziness.

Hyatt looked and looked again but saw nothing. Morse swung around, watched Hyatt a moment then said, 'You can't pick 'em up unless they're moving. Right now they're stopped out there. Reckon, since we're not scufflin' up any more dust, they're wondering where we went an' what we're up to.'

Morse was right. Hyatt saw the riders only when they moved out again. They were no longer bunched up, but now rode in an ever-widening company-front. 'Like soldiers,' he muttered. 'Skirmish order, Sheriff.' He looked around. 'They've figured out that since there's no more dust, we're no longer moving, which means to them we're finished; we're forted-up somewhere, waiting.'

'Wouldn't take a heap of sense to come to those conclusions,' growled Tom Morse, edging out for a look at the blazing, blurry land.

Hyatt said right back: 'No. And it doesn't take much sense to be able to pull a trigger either.'

Tom Morse shrugged. He was a man without delusions. A lot of Texans had met their Alamos, singly, in pairs, in little holed-up groups like this. A lot of them had never afterwards been found—Texas was a big country. He'd picked his profession and he'd been in tight spots before too. If he was to die here—all right. He wasn't going to do it gracefully or elegantly like a saint or a martyr because he was neither of these things; he was a Texas fighting-man, and no Texas fighting-man worth his salt ever died easy. He turned to say something about this frontier fatalism to Hyatt Tolman, but Tolman wasn't there.

Across the scooped-out centre of their natural fortress in the direction of Canebrake, were other places a man could secrete himself and keep a vigil. That's where Hyatt went. He had been a soldier lacking just four days of four long years—from Bull Run to Appomattox Court House. In a spot like this is wasn't difficult at all to revert to the ways of soldiers.

He knew, for instance, that within another hour at the most, Tonnahill's Mexicans would find him in his boulder-field with his friends and their prisoner. He also knew that those renegades were also experienced in this guerilla-type fighting; they wouldn't attack just Tom Morse's side of the rocks; they'd come like howling Commanches, from all directions, shooting and screaming and waving their cruel knives. Whether he and his companions survived the first charge depended upon just how fast and accurate they could shoot, but if they *did* roll back Tonnahill's marauders, it could, at best, be only a temporary thing.

He had thought that surely someone would have seen that fiercely burning shack last night. But no one had appeared hastening southward from the vicinity of Cancbrake to investigate. And that brush patch he'd fired—that had been another signal, another mute appeal for help. He raised up a little to look around, saw nothing up the northward plain and sank back down again. He was certain that brush-patch fire had been seen; its black-oily smoke had stood up into the faded brassy day like a flag. But there was still no one visible on the northward trace.

Loose stones rattled below, Hyatt looked out and down. Sam Hale grinned up at him and kept climbing until he could ease into the narrow crevice where Hyatt crouched holding his Winchester.

'Couldn't sleep anyway,' muttered the ranger. 'Too blamed hot.' He peered out, shrugged at the empty void and said, 'If we could hold 'em off until nightfall . . .'

Hyatt was shaking his head before Sam let it trickle off into silence. 'After nightfall they can sneak right up into these damned rocks, Ranger, poke their guns through and get us by just volley-firing.'

Hale thought on this, nodded and said, 'You're sure a cheerful cuss, Tolman.'

They exchanged a smile.

Man-sweat and passing time merged until, with the sun beginning to show pink pigment as it began its long glide downward across the frayed sky, Sheriff Morse whistled. He had seen something and was motioning to Hyatt and Sam Hale from across their stone-ringed stronghold, was making the hand-sign for a large Mexican sombrero. Hyatt waved back and Hale eased around to climb down into the centre of their fortress.

'I'll take the west wall,' he said to Hyatt; he said that matter-of-factly, like he might have said he was going for a drink of water. Hyatt watched him reach the ground, walk across where Jim Booth was lying, glance downward and walk on past. It occurred to Hyatt that with two like Hale and Morse, they just might survive the first attack, after all.

Chapter Seventeen

A little reddish-brown desert fox suddenly broke out of the rocks below Hyatt's vantage point and went running fleetly northward. Evidently this little scavenger had waited in his cool den in the boulders as long as he could, expecting the men to go away, had caught the

170

oncoming scent of many more men and had desperately fled in panic. This little animal reminded Hyatt of the dog. He turned and looked downward; Sam was over near their resting horses with his head on his paws, watching Jim Booth. He wasn't growling at Booth's strainings but neither was he wagging his tail. His expression put Hyatt in mind of one stranger analytically examining another stranger.

A long way out, and westward, someone fired a rifle or a carbine, at that distance it was difficult to tell from the report which it was, but one thing was certain, that man hadn't seen Hyatt or Sam or Tom. He'd probably, Hyatt surmised, walked up on to a rattlesnake out there in the brush; this rocky, sparse and barren land was ideal rattler country, especially being as hot and dry as it was.

The next gunshot though was much closer and Hyatt heard the bullet glance off stone over near Morse's vantage point and go wickedly whistling off overhead. Then Morse fired. No more than five seconds later Sam also fired. Hyatt twisted around, feeling left out.

Morse poked his head out and seeing Hyatt called across to him. 'They're sneakin' up on foot through the sage. They've got us figured out now.'

Tom had scarcely finished speaking when a ragged volley broke out along the south and west bastions of their boulder-jumble. Neither Sam nor Tom fired back. Hyatt, wishing to get into the fight, edged backwards to leave his crevice, which was fortunate, because a prone Mexican out in the brush fired upwards and the bullet struck stone, bounced across where Hyatt had been, struck stone again, and fell at his feet flattened to the size of a half dollar. He gazed from the slug to the distant patch of northward brush. He stopped backing away and waited a long time for sunlight to reflect off metal. Over along the west wall Sam Hale was hotly engaged now. Tom Morse, too, fired from time to time. Hyatt's Mexican brigand stealthily poked his Winchester barrel through the brush and took a long rest. Hyatt curved his right shoulder around the stock of his own Winchester, dropped his cheek, caught the lethal blaze of sunlight off metal across his front sight, and fired. The Mexican's gun went violently upwards. Behind it there was a violent threshing in the brush, then a gradual, quivering stillness. The shattered Winchester fell from a lifeless hand and lay exposed upon the gritty earth.

Someone was shouting in bad Spanish, giving orders, demanding a charge upon the rocks. Hyatt heard Tom Morse's thin curses above the gunshots and that railing voice. Tom evidently recognised, as Hyatt also did, that this insistent voice did not belong to a Mexican. But the man was nowhere in Hyatt's view, and as the voice died away, along with the gunfire around their fortress, Hyatt didn't think so much of Curly Tonnahill out there urging his men on, as he thought of the pretty girl and her baby back in Canebrake.

A lull ensued. Tom twisted around to softly call out. His face was beet-red and dripping sweat. 'They're goin' to rush us, boys. They're drawin' back to get set for a charge. Look sharp. This'll be it.'

Sam Hale, standing with his back half exposed and leaning forward to sight down the gunbarrel he had pushed through a slit in the rocks, turned and called out: 'Shoot low! Shoot low. Make 'em count!'

That was all Sam had time for. Beyond the rocks where the brush grew thickest, there was a barren width of earth perhaps twenty or thirty feet wide all around the rocks. If the Mexicans rushed out of the brush, and if they charged *en masse*, the defenders, hopelessly out-numbered but well armed and ready, would have to decimate them as they ran across that intervening area where there was no cover.

They could have perhaps faced this critical dilemma with equanimity had there been no more than eight or ten attackers, but against the horde of howling men arrayed against them, they could resolve only to do their utmost, and this is what they did.

That roaring voice back in the southward

173

brush was shouting encouragement in ungrammatical and profane Spanish. Sam suddenly opened up with his carbine. Hyatt, torn between rushing over to support Sam and not abandoning his own position, grew taut as Tom Morse also began to fire fiercely.

The Mexicans hadn't yet made their break. They were pouring volley after furious volley into the rocks. Ricocheting bullets made their evil scream and the air grew pungent with the stench of burnt gunpowder. The noise gradually increased until Hyatt's head was filled with it, leaving no room for thoughts of any kind.

Then he too was caught up in the vortex of battle.

Evidently the crafty Mexicans hadn't ever intended to rush Tom or Sam, across that stretch of open country. They had only intended to pin them down, intended to force them to fight for their lives where they were while the attackers made their wild rush from the north.

Hyatt saw the first man break through the underbrush, wave his carbine and let off a shout as he sprang ahead. This man's momentary pause and grand heroics cost him his life. Hyatt knocked him backwards into the brush with a plumb-centre hit. But the others were breaking through now, and these were men determined to get across the clearing only. They fired Winchesters and six-shooters from the hip in the general direction of Hyatt's narrow crevice, only hoping for a hit, but concerned more with diverting Hyatt, with driving him away with their shots until they could get across to the rocks where they could flatten or begin to scrabble around for a way inside.

He stubbornly refused to budge and worked the lever of his carbine until thc weapon sounded like an automatic weapon. When the Winchester was empty he used his sixgun. Because he was coldly determined, and also because the sweaty, frantic marauders came in a bunch, he cut them down in a wide swath. One Mexican, hard-hit, turned with a scream and hurled himself back through the brush. Hyatt had two bullets left in his .45 when this happened. Below his crevice were seven dead men whom the others stumbled over in their frantic haste. He caught the foremost Mexican squarely in the top of the head. This man fell like stone. Behind him another raider stumbled, nearly fell, lost his carbine and cried out for quarter. The men around this marauder, hearing that desperate appeal, turned suddenly and raced back the way they had come. Hyatt shot the kneeling Mexican as the man lunged for a pistol lying upon the ground. This was his last bullet, but in the bloody confusion below him, although guns were still going off, the men were breaking, were veering off left and right and running hard for some kind of shelter. He wasn't conscious of roaring imprecations at them until the noise began to subside, and he heard his own voice howling grisly epithets in Spanish.

Elsewhere too, the gunfire began to lessen, to dwindle off to occasional wild shots. Men's loud groans and pleas for water, for succour, took over where the gunfire quit. Hyatt was panting although he hadn't moved, his throat was ash-dry and his eyes burnt. He began systematically to re-load both his guns and the farther around his shell belt his groping fingers went in search of bullets, the more it was driven home to him that one more charge like that one, and he would have to use his carbine as a club because there would be no more bullets to feed it.

For nearly fifteen minutes there was no gunfire at all. It seemed that the raiders had withdrawn deep into the brush for a council, or to care for their injured. Tom Morse, his salt-stiff shirt dark with perspiration, hatless and red-eyed, stepped back into the centre of their stronghold. Sam Hale remained up there on his improvised cat-walk with his re-loaded Winchester lying in its slot, but he also turned to look downward and around. Hyatt made a tired little signal to the others that he was still unhurt. They made the same signal back again. Jim Booth had chewed through his neckerchief-gag; his bold eyes were fixed incredulously upon Hyatt. He was the only one who spoke.

'You fools, they'll get you sure. Call for Tonnahill. Get him to lead his damned greasers far enough away so we can make a run for it.'

Hyatt gazed at Booth. 'There's a pile of dead ones below my position against the rocks,' he said. 'If Tonnahill even suggested that the Mexicans pull back, they'd kill him on the spot. But even if we could get 'em away, we couldn't get a mile on those horses. Use your head, Booth.'

'*Use my head!*' exploded the lanky outlaw, straining against his bonds. 'Tolman; we're all goin' to be massacred in here!'

Sheriff Morse coughed, spat dust, and said in a gravelly tone of voice, 'Better here where we got some chance at least, than a mile from here where there's no cover at all. Now shut up, Booth.'

Booth didn't shut up, he swung towards Morse, still fighting his bonds, and cried out, 'Then set me loose and give me a gun. Damned if I like the idea of dyin' trussed up like a lousy turkey!'

Sam Hale made a flinty laugh. 'That's just exactly what we need in here—you turned loose with a gun.' Sam swung to briefly glance out into the heathazed near distance, then put his back to the rocks again and gazed from Hyatt to Sheriff Morse. He didn't say anything to the other two; there actually wasn't anything to say. There was no way to deploy their forces for a better defence and there was nothing to joke about. As for idle conversation, it was not only inappropriate here, it was also difficult; like the others, Sam's throat was raw from burnt powder, rock-dust and dehydration.

Tom Morse went back to his position, crouched down and wormed in where he'd left his carbine. Hyatt turned and also resumed the watch, but there was nothing to see. Below him a Mexican was softly whimpering. He risked peeking straight downwards to locate that man, failed to find him and pulled back.

Somewhere over in front of Sam Hale a sniper opened up. Sam didn't reply. This sniper would fire, roll away from where the little puff of tell-tale dirty smoke drifted up, and fire again. Sam replied only once, and after that the sniper was quiet for a long while as he crawled northward, got into position again, and threw a bullet upwards towards Hyatt's crevice.

Hyatt accepted this personal challenge to combat but, like Sam, wishing to conserve bullets, didn't shoot because he couldn't be certain of a hit. The sniper spent a half hour trying his hardest to score, but caution kept him too far back in the brush patch. Hyatt eventually came to accept those intermittent gunshots and ignored them. The moaning man down below him finally became quiet. He undoubtedly had bled out and died.

Time ran on; other raiders skulked up close in the brush to snipe. Their bullets chipped the rock and the danger was more from these unpredictable flying, razor-sharp slivers of granite, than it was from the bullets themselves.

A man's voice lifted through a sudden long hush, calling out in hoarse English for Tolman and the beseiged peace officers to surrender or be wiped out. The second this demand had been made Tom Morse blistered the unseen man, who had to be Curly Tonnahill, with sizzling imprecations, and dared him to show himself.

Tonnahill called back in the same husky voice, saying, 'You old fool. Do you think you're goin' to get out of this alive?'

'No,' roared back the angry sheriff, 'and I hope those pepper-bellies with you wake up to the fact that it's you who's got that stagecoach money cached away, and that they'll gain nothing by killing us except to maybe lose another ten or twelve men.'

Tonnahill called Morse a fighting name, then he said, 'Have you fellers got Jim Booth in there with you?'

'We have,' bellowed Morse. 'If you want him—just walk on in here an' take him.'

'Turn Booth loose,' said Tonnahill.

Sam Hale sounded off with a harsh laugh. 'Sure we will. We'll turn him loose the same time those Mexicans with you hand you over to us with your arms lashed behind you. Otherwise, do like Sheriff Morse says, walk on in an' get him.'

Tonnahill tried a new tack. 'Who's in there besides Jim Booth?'

'Davy Crockett,' sang out Sam derisively, 'Jim Bowie, Will Travis, Ol' Man Maverick; you name 'em, Tonnahill, an' anyone else you can think of. If you doubt me, come on out where you can count your casualties.'

Tonnahill called Hale a savage name. 'You think this is a joke, mister, just hang an' rattle; you're goin' to find out just how funny it is in a few minutes. You're goin' to laugh yourself to death!'

Hyatt, quiet through this angry exchange, climbed down and walked over to Booth. Whatever Tonnahill was up to, he'd as well as promised he wouldn't be ready for a short while yet, and Hyatt wanted an answer to a question concerning Tonnahill which had been bothering him ever since he'd helped deliver that baby girl.

Booth glared upwards. Fifty feet away the dog eyed Hyatt and gently swept the ground with his tail. 'What d'you want?' Booth snarled, sweat running off him in rivulets. 'If you think I can talk Curly into anything, guess again.'

Hyatt leaned upon his carbine. 'Did Curly ever mention a wife to you fellers at the goat-ranch, Booth?'

Booth's eyes widened, then turned crafty. 'You tryin' to pull something?' he demanded suspiciously. 'A wife? Curly Tonnahill? Don't be silly, Tolman. He's got no wife. Who'd be burdened with a wife?'

'A girl then; did he even mention having a girl along when he hit that stage?'

'Hell, no. Tolman, if you're tryin' to pull something, forget it.' Booth turned his head and Hyatt had his answer. The girl—and the baby—belonged to Tonnahill all right, but they didn't mean a thing to him, which is all Hyatt wished to be certain of.

Booth growled under his breath: 'A wife! Of all the silly damned fool . . .' He swung his venomous gaze back around. 'Try something betten'n that, Tolman, if you're hatchin' something.'

Hyatt shrugged. 'I'm not trying anything, Booth. He brought a girl to the Canebrake country with him, hid her in a shack in a hidden canyon and abandoned her there. She was goin' to have a baby. I happened along and helped her have it.'

'So,' snarled the lanky outlaw, 'he had a girl, and the damned thing had a baby. What of it?'

'Behind that shack is an old cave, Booth. You said Curly didn't have the stage loot with him when he arrived at the goat-ranch.'

Booth's pale gaze turned speculative, turned craftily thoughtful as he continued to stare

181

upwards. 'The money's in the cave?' he asked quietly.

Hyatt shook his head. 'I don't know. I think that's where it's got to be if he didn't have it on him.'

'You know where this cave is?'

'I just told you I did.'

Booth licked his lips. 'Set me loose, Tolman. Throw down on those damned lawmen. I swear to you Curly and I'll see to it the greasers don't massacre 'em. We'll split three ways.'

Hyatt regarded lanky Jim Booth stonily. 'Now who's being silly,' he said. 'You know damned well you're not going to walk out of this, and maybe I won't either, so who cares about that money?'

Chapter Eighteen

It began to appear to Hyatt Tolman as time ran on, that Curly Tonnahill's Mexican allies weren't enthusiastic about rushing the stronghold again. Occasionally a few snipers slipped up through the brush and tried to catch a glimpse of the Texans, but after six or eight near misses, Morse and Hyatt and the ranger kept well clear.

Finally, Tonnahill came back to call forward again, this time sounding less than confident.

He said, 'Hey; you fellers forted up in the rocks, listen to me: I got a proposition for you. Walk out, leave your horses, money, and Jim Booth behind, and the Messicans have agreed they'll let you go. You got my word for it too.'

'Your word,' sang out Tom Morse, 'isn't worth the breath required to give it . . . Tonnahill? What's the matter; your pepper-bellies run out of guts? Come on, rush us again. We're re-loaded and waitin'.'

Tonnahill swore savagely. 'All right,' he exclaimed loudly. 'Have it your way. All we've got to do is wait you out. You can't sneak out, your water'll be runnin' low directly, and come nightfall, we'll sneak up barefoot and slit your lousy throats. There's no moon, remember, lawman.'

Sam Hale said, 'Hey, Tonnahill; how long you expect those Mexicans to stand around like this, losin' men and gettin' nothing for it? They'll cut *your* throat before this is over. You wait'n see.'

Hyatt, listening to these angry exchanges and keeping a watch on his part of the onward land, suddenly saw something that momentarily stopped his breath. A very faint, distantly vague shadowing of dun colouring beating upwards in an unusually long line from east to west, far back upon the northward range. Hope sprang up in his heart; when he wanted to turn and cry out exultantly to the others with him, though, good sense kept him

183

from it. If it was a mirage up there, or if his red-rimmed, weary and watering eyes were playing tricks on him, there was no point in disappointing Hale and Morse too.

Then a sniper fired down below in the brush and a bullet chipped the rock within six inches of him, forcing him to crouch low and return to rummaging the closer land for this deadly enemy. But he didn't see the sniper; he hadn't so far seen any of those wraith-like gunmen out there in the shimmering heat.

Now though, the Mexicans had recovered from their earlier rout and by their stiffening gunfire showed that they were surrounding the rock pile again, sneaking up close into the brush and firing again. Now, too, it appeared that they had at last worked out a sound strategy.

They knew by this time that there were only three men inside the rocks. They also knew there were four sides to that natural fortress. Simple arithmetic left them with an obvious conclusion; regardless of which of the defenders moved off to face the exposed position, there would always be one part of the rock pile unprotected.

Hyatt saw at once what Tonnahill had in mind. So also did Ranger Hale and Sheriff Morse. Tom called a warning, but by then it was unnecessary. Bullets began coming into the rocks from along the eastern wall where that pathway led inside, the same passageway they had used to get inside the boulders. Hyatt anxiously tried to watch his frontal brush patch and that interior debouchement of the pathway too, but eventually, as more and more marauders infiltrated the brush patch, stepping up their gunfire, he was limited to only very brief backward glimpses.

He had now quite forgotten that mirage-like, distant cloud of dust off in the shimmering north.

Tom Morse roared a warning. Hyatt whipped around in time to see Hale shoot point-blank at a burly Mexican who suddenly materialised in the pathway's innermost opening. The Mexican threw out his arms and went down. Sam, whose back was exposed to the inside of their stronghold, didn't turn back to face westward again, but kept watch on the passageway directly across from him. This of course did precisely what the attackers had figured it would; it left the west wall temporarily unguarded.

Hyatt tried to twist around enough so that he could at least partially cover Sam's western perimeter. He failed, though, because the Mexicans creeping towards him through the brush out front, got bolder as their numbers increased.

The gunfire seemed to grow and swell towards an unbelievable crescendo. Men's shouts and outcries sounded dimly through it. The noise kept increasing until Hyatt, swinging his head to dash away sweat, thought that each raider must be firing two guns. Still the noise increased. Hyatt was bewildered. Lead struck all around his crevice. He sucked back a little and risked a look backwards over towards the pathway. It was empty and Sam was still up there on his granite parapet keeping watch. Hyatt turned back into the face of that deafening, unprecedented gun-thunder, and caught a glimpse of rigid Mexicans down there in the brush standing straight up and twisting around. He raised his carbine, snugged it back, then didn't fire. Two Mexicans in plain sight suddenly pitched forward and fell across sage plants. Two more spun around and fired backwards into the brush behind them. A shrill rebel yell burst out far back somewhere. Hyatt lifted his cheek to peer beyond his front sight. The Mexicans were now all crying out to one another, and although they had just about stopped firing altogether, that rattling thunder of guns did not diminish. Finally, Hyatt saw several bobbing, weaving heads; they were not adorned with the immense sombreros of Mexico, but instead showed the felt hats and much narrower brims of frontier Texas. Hyatt knew, finally, that the cloud of dust he'd seen earlier hadn't been a mirage after all; that somehow, during the fierce fighting, reinforcements for the besieged men had arrived behind the Mexicans from Canebrake.

He raised his head and answered that rebel

yell with another howl just like it. The attacking raiders were now trying to flee westward, but out there the roar of guns blew up into a deafening dirge and more Texas-hats began to appear throughout the underbrush.

Tom Morse jumped up into plain view and waved his hat and his red-hot carbine. It was a foolish and reckless thing to do. Sam Hale was the last defender to realise that help had arrived. Even after he saw a Texan down inside the rocks waving his arms for Sam not to shoot, the ranger still held his carbine levelled, his body stiff and poised for resistance.

Dust beat upwards far out where horsemen were converging from the reddening west upon the distant spot where Tonnahill's men had left their mounts. For another long five minutes that raging battle continued, then it began to dwindle as Mexican marauders threw down their weapons and cried out for quarter.

Finally, an occasional shot sounded, far out, but in closer, the fighting was ended.

Tom Morse jumped down inside the stronghold yelling at Hale and Hyatt Tolman. 'The men from Canebrake,' he said over and over again, his unshaven, red-eyed, dirty face shining in a big sweaty grin. 'The boys from town; we're goin' out of here standin' up after all. Hey, Sam—Hyatt—we made it through alive!'

Hyatt got stiffly down and met Sam Hale

where the ranger reached the inner compound. Tom Morse rushed towards them, then halted with his mouth wide open, his bulging eyes falling upon Booth. The lanky outlaw was leaning peacefully against a boulder, his head sunk forward on to his chest. Sam Hale said, 'A Mex jumped through the passageway yonder. He shot the same time I shot him. But he saw only Booth, not me. He must've figured Booth was one of us.'

Tom dropped his arms, bent slightly from the waist and squinted. 'Smack-dab between the eyes,' he said. 'Booth never knew what struck him.'

Across where that inward trail lay, several men came stepping along gingerly, guns up and heads moving. Hyatt recognised one of them right off: Simpson Franklin, the cattleman from the Canebrake country who had caught him in the cabin with Tonnahill's wife. Hyatt made a half-hearted gesture of greeting. Franklin nodded and led the other men on over. Just before the two parties came together Hyatt stepped ahead to Franklin.

'There was a white man—a Texan named Tonnahill—with the Mexicans. Did you see him?'

Franklin recognised Hyatt and nodded. 'Yeah; we seen him. He's lyin' about a hundred yards out front of that little trail we come in by. He's bad off; if you got anythin' to say you'd better hurry, mister.'

Hyatt nodded, ducked around the men with Franklin, who eyed him with lively interest, and hastened on out on to the reddening plain.

He found Tonnahill; there were four curious men leaning upon their rifles watching the outlaw die. They gazed at Hyatt as he came up, knelt and cradled the strange outlaw's head in his lap. Tonnahill had two bulletholes in him, one in thc left breast, one in the right breast. He probably felt no pain, just a gathering numbness, but he was bleeding internally. There was no hope at all for him. He knew it; it showed in the steady, dull way he looked straight up into Hyatt's face.

'Curly,' Hyatt said. 'The stage money—it's in the cave, isn't it?'

Tonnahill made a shallow cough; claret bubbled past the corner of his mouth. 'Any chance?' he whispered.

'None,' said Hyatt. 'You got two in the lights.'

'Yeah, stranger, it's hid in the cave.' Tonnahill struggled to rally. 'You know about the cave . . . ?'

'I saw it. I helped your girl have her baby.'

'You—did? Damned female anyway . . . what a hell of a time too . . .' Tonnahill coughed again, this time the blood gushed. He rolled his head weakly. 'Sure gettin' dark,' he whispered.

Hyatt said no more. He held the outlaw until he died, then eased him down gently,

189

stood up and looked at the solemn-eyed Texans motionlessly standing there. 'He's the man who robbed your stagecoach up above Canebrake, and when we get back I'll show you where he hid the money.'

One of those Texans gravely eyed the dead outlaw, then said, 'You're that feller Tom Morse had in jail for the robbery ain't you, mister?'

Hyatt nodded.

The Texan shifted his gaze, saying, ' 'That there your dog, mister?'

Hyatt turned and looked around. Sam was standing behind him, his tongue lolling, his long tail gently wagging. He put down a hand and let it lie atop Sam's head. 'He's my dog, yes.'

The impassive, craggy cowman nodded. 'Been through a heap more'n most dogs go through,' he stated, and looked straight at Hyatt. 'By the way, your little lady at the hotel asked us fellers when we was organisin' to come down here last night an' see what'n hell was goin' on, to sort of look out for you.'

'*My* little lady . . . ?'

The Texans eyed Hyatt steadily and that same older man nodded his head. 'Yeah; she said she belonged to you—if she belonged to anyone at all, mister. Well; wasn't she tellin' the truth?'

Hyatt smiled softly. 'She was tellin' the truth,' he said. The older man squinted over where Tom Morse and Sam Hale, amid a crowd of other men, came leading their horses out of the stronghold. He said, 'Mister; is one of them horses the one you was ridin'?'

Hyatt nodded again, glancing around.

The cowman brought his sombre glance back. 'Well, I'll tell you,' he drawled. 'Ain't none of them horses goin' to carry a feller back to town as fast as you got to get there, so I'll loan you my critter. You can leave him at the liverybarn. I'll pick him up later.'

Hyatt studied this craggy old rangeman. 'I'll wait,' he said, 'and return with the rest of you. Two, three more hours won't make that much difference.'

But the older man shook his head about this. 'Let me tell you something,' he said quietly, his voice softening, turning deep and gentle. 'Menfolk're always ridin' off, an' sometimes they don't come ridin' back. You take my horse. That little lady's too young an' scairt to make her wait another few hours, mister. An' she's far too pretty too.' The cowman turned towards his listening companions. 'How about it?' he asked.

The other men agreed, some with words, some with little hard nods of their heads. One of them, undoubtedly thinking he knew how Hyatt's thoughts were running, said, 'Don't worry about this mess down here, stranger; we got all the live greasers rounded up, and the dead ones can wait—they're not goin'

191

anywhere until we can fetch back wagons for 'em. As for the rest of it—look at Sheriff Morse over there. He's talkin' a mile a minute. He can do all the explaining. We'll tell him where you went.'

The older man took Hyatt's arm in a rough but gentle grip, turned and led him off where several dozing horses stood in the care of several other heavily armed Texans. He took one horse from this bunch, passed the reins over to Hyatt, and, still without smiling or changing expression at all, said, 'About your baby, mister; I always sort of cottoned to namin' after their mothers. That is, o' course, unless you already got a name picked out.'

Hyatt stepped up over leather, gripped the old cowman's rough paw, dropped it as he gathered the reins, and said, 'You're plumb right, pardner. They always ought to be named after their mother.'

He waved and loped away heading northward towards Canebrake, in the quiet, red late afternoon with a freshening breath of early-evening coolness cooling his face and reviving his spirits. Twenty feet back Sam the big old shaggy dog ran along behind him. Once, Hyatt turned to look back. It didn't seem right, he told himself, to raise a little girl without a dog for her to rely on as well as a new pappy.

We hope you have enjoyed this Large Print book. Other Chivers Press or Thorndike Press Large Print books are available at your library or directly from the publishers.

For more information about current and forthcoming titles, please call or write, without obligation, to:

Chivers Large Print
published by BBC Audiobooks Ltd
St James House, The Square
Lower Bristol Road
Bath BA2 3BH
UK
email: bbcaudiobooks@bbc.co.uk
www.bbcaudiobooks.co.uk

OR

Thorndike Press
295 Kennedy Memorial Drive
Waterville
Maine 04901
USA
www.gale.com/thorndike
www.gale.com/wheeler

All our Large Print titles are designed for easy reading, and all our books are made to last.